Infinityglass

Also by Myra McEntire

hourglass

timepiece
An Hourglass Novel

Infinityglass

An Hourglass Novel

Myra McEntire

EGMONT
USA
New York

EGMONT

We bring stories to life

First published by Egmont USA, 2013
443 Park Avenue South, Suite 806
New York, NY 10016

Copyright © Myra McEntire, 2013
All rights reserved

1 3 5 7 9 8 6 4 2

www.egmontusa.com
http://myramcentire.blogspot.com/

Library of Congress Cataloging-in-Publication Data is available.
LCCN number: 2013937007

ISBN 978-1-60684-441-0
eBook ISBN 978-1-60684-442-7

Printed in the United States of America

To Ethan, Andrew, and Charlie:
I owe you a year

To Stephanie Perkins: TWYLA

*"The only person you are destined to become
is the person you decide to be."*

—Ralph Waldo Emerson

Chapter 1

Hallie, September, New Orleans

"The only reason you want my help is so you can see my girls in a corset," I said.

"Hallie. Keep it real." Poe rolled his eyes. "I know those aren't yours."

I launched a thigh-high boot at his head but missed, leaving a black mark on my bedroom wall.

Poe Sharpe was built like a spark plug, compact and hard, with an imperfect face that always made girls take a second look. Probably as they tried to figure out why he was attractive. I chalked it up to his smile, his swagger, and an unhealthy amount of leather.

"Why can't you just pop in and be done with the whole thing?" I asked.

"You have to distract the front man so I can get the job done," Poe answered, with a fair amount of tolerance for all the bitching I was doing.

"I'm just saying," I grumbled as I laced up the other boot, "that there's no point in being able to teleport if you still need a sidekick. I could be doing something more useful." And more exciting.

"Don't call it teleporting. It maxes out my geek factor." He pushed away from the wall. "And I like to think of you as my companion."

"Only if I get to be Amy Pond."

"Who?"

I sighed. "How can you call yourself British and not know who—"

"Hurry up. You know how he gets when we aren't on time." He was referring to Paul Girard, who didn't like to be kept waiting by anyone, especially his daughter.

"Out." I pointed at my door. "I need to finish getting dressed, and I'm not putting on a free show here."

"Even if I drop a couple of dollars?"

"Not even if you make it rain."

Grinning, he tossed my boot back and headed downstairs to my father's office, whistling, "Brown Eyed Girl."

My eyes were hazel.

Poe and I had started circling each other the day we met two years ago. He carried his sexy in a dangerous way. Bonus, he could teleport right into my bedroom. By the time my dad caught us in a "delicate" situation, we'd discovered we were better friends than friends with benefits. The fact that my dad allowed Poe to walk out of our house alive that night confirmed his worth. A regular guy would've left in a body bag.

I continued lacing my boot while staring at my lips in the mirror, concentrating on making them bigger, smaller, wider, thinner. I'd learned how to go chameleon and stay that way when I was twelve. My body was considerably top-heavy for the next couple of years, but there was no one around to impress. No one appropriate, anyway. Holding a different shape for too long made me tired, and the novelty wore off, so now, at seventeen, I looked like me unless I was on a job. Barely a B cup.

I could transmutate, much like Mystique of *X-Men* fame, but with zero blue skin and much better hair. Of course, her boobs reigned superior. My cells didn't follow the same rules of time everyone else's did. They regenerated constantly. I could speed them up or slow them down, manipulate them into different shapes, sizes, even colors. Handy in a pinch. Or in a theft.

Today's mark was Skeevy's Pawnshop. All the intelligence I'd gathered—in a different meat suit each time—supported the fact that the shop perfectly fit its name. Dusty glass cases held jewelry, firearms, guitars—the usual pawnshop fodder. They also displayed the forsaken dreams the items represented, but those outlines weren't quite as clear.

Through the back door of Skeevy's existed a mysterious space that rivaled the Vatican's secret archives. Instead of papal secrets, it housed much trashier cousins.

Tonight, Poe and I were responsible for stealing one of its most prized items and delivering it to my father.

Type *Paul Girard* into a search engine, and you could find anything from white lies to blatant truths. Rumors that he was a mob boss, a drug lord, or an arms dealer.

In truth, he headed up a worldwide conglomerate: Girard Industries. Privately funded, with anonymous investors and elusive headquarters. Or as legit as my father could go and still make the kind of money to which he'd become accustomed.

Girard Industries' enormous umbrella hid one business in particular.

Chronos.

Add to this the suggestion of my dad's gangster reputation, the rumors that swirled about how honest his business practices were, and the amount of enemies he'd created in the past twenty years, and the sum equaled bodyguards and fear and my ivory-tower life. The only time Dad let me out of the house without a bodyguard was to do jobs for Chronos, and even then he had a security detail on me 50 percent of the time. No better way to manipulate a daddy than by putting his little girl on the firing line.

More than one hit had been put out on Paul Girard. Only one had been put out on me. My transmutation gene had allowed my body to heal before I bled out.

Others hadn't been so lucky.

My phone chirped, and without looking, I knew it was Poe

texting from my dad's office, telling me to hurry. I pulled on a T-shirt over my corset and taffeta tutu and headed downstairs.

Once Dad learned about things like time travel, teleportation, remote viewing, and psychometry, it wasn't a huge leap for him to figure out the best way to use them. He was the leading dealer in the "special" artifacts black market. I could've called him a magical mafia boss, but I wouldn't. Not to his face, anyway.

Poe and I were partners. He could teleport. I could change my appearance, change it again, and change it some more. He could get in and out of places quickly. I could gather intel, ask questions, and cause distractions, all in a hundred different disguises.

There were veils in the fabric of time. Poe once compared them to waiting rooms for wormholes, and they were his conduits to teleporting in and out of places. I could see them, like solid walls of water in the atmosphere, but only Poe could get into them, which meant I had to take a lot of cabs.

I found my ability infinitely more valuable than Poe's, but my father didn't seem to agree.

"The guy behind the counter will be alone," Dad said. "Hallie will distract him. You'll handle everything else."

Even though he'd made a point of waiting for me to walk through his office door to go over the rundown of tonight's activities, Dad spoke directly to Poe, like I wasn't even in the room.

"Why does Poe always take care of the big stuff?" I asked.

A lesser woman might be too intimidated to speak up, but

when you went through puberty with Paul Girard for a father and no mother as a buffer, tough was a by-product. He would accept nothing less.

He ignored me and kept talking to Poe. "You're the only one I want in the back of the shop."

"Yes, sir," Poe said. I'd never seen him be subservient to anyone except for my father, and it was because my dad was a scary mother trucker.

Even so, subservience wasn't in my repertoire. I resented playing the part of the sidekick again, and Dad knew it. I wanted to *make sure* he knew it.

Dad continued, "All the scouting work we did—"

I interrupted. "You mean, all the scouting work *I* did."

Dad's dark-eyed stare was created to intimidate, and his mere presence was effective enough to sway most people into going along with anything he said, but I wasn't backing down.

"Taking the watch shouldn't be a problem," he said to Poe, "as long as you port in."

I put my hands on my hips. "Well, he isn't going to *walk in.*"

"Then you port to the agreed-upon location," he finished.

"Which is where?" I asked.

"Doesn't matter." Dad landed his eagle eyes on me. "You'll take a cab home."

"Tell me, Dad. Do you dismiss everything I say because you're sexist or because you think I'm stupid?"

Wisely, Poe backed into a corner to stay out of the line of fire.

"Your level of respect is inappropriate." Dad's jaw was clenching.

"When do I ever do anything that *is* appropriate?" I asked.

"If you want to do this job, I would suggest you start immediately."

I knew from Dad's jaw and the tightness around his eyes that I'd pushed him too far. Now wasn't the time to challenge him unless I wanted to get rolled over, and I wasn't about to lose the chance to leave the house.

"Yes, sir." I dropped my head.

And today's round goes to Alpha Daddy.

Poe didn't say a word as we walked out of Dad's office, but his look clearly indicated I should've shut up way before I did.

My look back indicated he should screw off.

"He only acts that way because he loves you," Poe said.

"So ignoring me equals loving me?"

"It does when it means he's scared."

I grabbed my bag and headed for the front door. Even though I preferred it, taking Dad's town car wasn't the best way to stay undercover. A cab waited at the corner, and I climbed in and gave the address. The driver didn't balk when I pulled off my oversized T-shirt and adjusted the laces on my corset. New Orleans cab drivers were tough to rattle.

I'd figured out the art of decadent camouflage. Thanks to the number of flamboyant visitors to the clubs on Bourbon, I found it easy to blend in the Quarter. I had one rule when it came to my disguises: Go hard or go home. Dressing up gave me a chance to step into someone else's fictitious life. Sometimes my characters had elaborate backstories. Other times, the simplicity of the costume sufficed.

I gave my makeup one last check in my compact mirror. Tonight, it involved glitter, false eyelashes with feathers on the ends, and lots of glittery powder in my fake cleavage. My blue wig topped it all off, perfectly and literally. I slicked my mouth with bright pink lip gloss for the finishing touch, and tapped the back of the cabbie's seat once we hit the edge of the French Quarter. I gave him the fare plus twenty bucks.

"You never saw me, right?"

From the way he looked at my chest, he'd seen way more of me than I'd wanted.

My platform boots gave me a definite swagger, and my taffeta tutu accentuated the swing of my hips. I focused on the ground and concentrated on lengthening the shape of my eyelids, along with puffing up my lips and making my cheekbones more prominent. I searched for my reflection and found it in a plate-glass window. I could see my own face underneath, but only because I was looking.

It had rained most of the day and a fine mist hung in the air, but the endless party still went strong. I melted into the crowd, noting details for my escape route, since I'd be on foot.

I couldn't always tell the bums from the tourists, and even though Mardi Gras was only one week a year, some glassy-eyed coed was always ready to lift her shirt for a string of cheap plastic beads. Stories were ripe for the picking in the Quarter, and most were written all over their authors' faces. The same creepy-ass clown stood outside Oz, juggling shot glasses tonight. I skirted my way past him without making eye contact.

I hated clowns.

I hooked a right down a side street. More warning than beacon, Skeevy's neon sign shone red off the wet payment. I straightened my shoulders and headed for the front door. Heavy metal bars covered the bulletproof windows. An electronic ding sounded my entry as I pushed open the door. Easy to get in, harder to leave, especially if you held something in your hands.

Good thing Poe would be taking a shortcut.

The register was the old-fashioned kind with ticker tape and a little bell that rang when the drawer opened. Cash only at Skeevy's. Checks bounced and credit cards left records, and no one on either side of the counter wanted that.

Danny Launoux was my target.

Thanks to my rock star surveillance skills, I knew he liked comics, vodka, and girls. That last part was crucial to my role in this little drama.

He wore 1970s, tinted glasses that didn't hide his eyes but did make him look like a pimp. The heels of his boots hung on the rungs of the stool where he sat hunched over, reading a *Batman* comic. A set of keys dangled from a chain on his belt. His hair was out of control, frizzy, curly, and more tall than wide. I forced fifty product suggestions to stay on the tip of my tongue and crossed the dirty, tan carpet. Danny didn't look up until I reached him. I waited for a reaction. I didn't get one.

"I'm looking for a ring," I said. It had been one of my mother's. I'd sold it earlier in the week as a blonde with thin lips, all Broke College Student Who Needed Tuition. I'd even managed tears. He hadn't been impressed then, either.

"Prices are on the tags. No bargaining. What you see is what you pay."

I browsed. Poe was already supposed to be in the back, but I couldn't be sure until I got confirmation. I checked my phone as I slinked toward the jewelry cases. No texts.

I made a big show of bending over, and then arched my back and stretched. I'd at least expected curiosity from Danny, but he'd gone back to reading. I dropped my arms to my sides with a sigh and tried the direct approach.

"Is that the latest *Batman* issue from the New 52 series?" My Internet research had told me all I needed to know about the 2011 relaunch of DC Comics. It had also lured me into placing an order of my own.

He blinked, lowered the comic, looked at me, looked at the cover, and then at me again. "That's what it says."

"I feel sorry for Batman. I couldn't imagine what it would be like to have to hide your identity. Never to be truly close to a woman. I like to get close. Don't you?"

"I don't care how hot you are. I'm not going to lower my prices because you're coming on to me," Danny said in a monotone. Definitely not distracted. More like bored.

Damn. I'd hoped my fierce comics knowledge would work in my favor in case my flirting didn't. "I'm not coming—"

"I know how women are," he said in a Cajun drawl. "And I could smell you angling for a deal when you walked in the door."

He could *smell* me? Jackass. I hated to use my sexuality for evil, and here he was, trivializing my effort.

"I happen to like *Batman*, and I told you, I want a ring. Show me the blue one."

He dropped his reading material with a sigh and slammed the side of his fist into the register drawer. It popped open, and he fished a set of keys from underneath a stack of twenties. If he could open the register with nothing less than a punch and wasn't afraid to let a customer know it, he wasn't worried about what was in the cash drawer. This confirmed his main concern was for whatever lurked behind the vaulted door on the far wall.

It was certainly mine.

"Is that a blue topaz?" I asked.

He squinted at the ring in question. "Aquamarine."

I checked my phone again as Danny leaned over to open the case. Nothing from Poe. An uneasy feeling stirred in the pit of my stomach.

Danny cleared his throat, and I realized he was holding

out the ring for me. I dropped my phone into my bag. "How much?"

"Three hundred and fifty."

Broke College Me had let it go for a hundred.

I took the ring and held it up to the light. "Do you have an appraisal?"

He snorted. "Hello. You're in a pawnshop."

"Who sold it to you?" I asked.

"We have a privacy policy."

I didn't budge.

He looked from me to the ring and back again. "Two hundred."

"Is that how much you paid for it?"

"Two. That's the price."

"Fine." I dug around in my bag under the pretense of looking for my wallet so I could check my phone again. My heart did a flip when I saw Poe's name on my screen.

I opened the message.

Help.

You knew you were in deep when someone who could teleport needed an escape plan.

"Uh-oh."

Danny raised his eyebrows.

"My . . . my date cancelled." I fought to keep my voice from shaking.

I flipped through my mental catalog, and recalled the details of the building schematic I'd stolen, trying to think of all the places Poe could be.

Danny took the ring out of my hand. "You were meeting your date at a pawnshop?"

"I have a busy schedule."

I watched a red light flash in the reflection from Danny's glasses. I knew it was from a surveillance camera that hung suspended from the ceiling, observing the happenings in the front of the shop. The blinking light was a sign that there was trouble in the back. What had Poe gotten himself into?

"I need to close up. Now."

"But the ring." I gestured toward it when he began to put it back in the case. "Your sign says, 'Open twenty-four hours,' and the ring—"

"We'll be open again at ten A.M." His voice was firm. "Come back then."

I huffed. "Your customer service is terrible."

"Complain to the management. There's a suggestion box. Outside."

My cell screen lit up the inside of my purse:

911 GET ME OUT 911

Poe was not an all-caps kind of guy.

Desperate now, I held up one finger and tossed my blue hair over my shoulders. "Does the NOLA PD know what you keep behind that big door?"

Danny looked at the flashing light on the camera once

more before he shoved the ring back into the case. "You don't need to worry about what's behind that door. You just need to leave. Now." He came out from behind the counter and cupped my elbow in his hand, trying to steer me out of the store.

Nothing pissed me off more than being manhandled. Unless I'd asked to be.

"Let go of me." I jerked away and clutched my arm. "That hurt."

"Does a hundred-dollar ring really mean so much that you can't come back to get it tomorrow?"

"You said two hundred!"

"You're familiar, somehow. You haven't been in here before, have you?" He squinted and lifted up his glasses like an old man. "I know your voice. . . ."

The one thing I hadn't figured out how to do was manipulate my vocal cords.

Shock and surprise broke through my concentration, and I could feel my disguise slip a little. Danny blinked in recognition. "Wait a second. You sold me the ring! What the hell is going on?"

A cell phone on the counter began to vibrate, and the accompanying ringtone was a repeating air horn. Danny turned around, and I did the only logical thing I could. I picked up the stool from behind the register and hit him over the head with it.

I didn't put all my strength into the move, because unlike my father, I didn't make murder a hobby. Danny still went down hard.

Once I knew he was out, I took his key ring off his belt. I navigated my fingers through his hair to get to his skull. Big knot, no blood, nothing concave.

He was probably fine.

I took the ring from the case, left a hundred-dollar bill in its place, and then dropped it into my bag. Once I found the right key, I opened the vault door and pulled it closed behind me. A corridor stretched thirty feet before taking a sharp right turn. Strobe lights near the ceiling signaled a silent alarm.

If any cameras existed, they were well hidden. I let my face and body go back to their natural state. When I reached the turn, I took a quick listen before peeking around the corner. I'd expected some sort of chaos, or at least a guard. All I saw was more tunnel.

I went farther and farther as the strobe lights continued to pulse. The lack of windows made the walls close in and tripped off a rare bout of claustrophobia. By the time I reached the next open space, my chest was tight. Even though I was freezing, sweat trickled down my back. Once again, I listened before turning the corner. Good thing.

Voices echoed against the slick surfaces of the walls and floors. One was Poe's; I could tell by the lilt of his English accent. The other was male and cocky.

"I won't tell anyone what you have here," Poe said. "You can just let me go."

"Someone already knows what I have or you wouldn't be

here." A lighter flicked, and a shadow appeared on the wall across from me. "Paul Girard sent you."

Cigarette smoke wafted toward me, and my body shook with the effort to stay still.

"We've discussed joining forces, but couldn't reach agreeable terms. He leans too far toward greed for my comfort."

Join forces, my ass. My dad didn't play well with others.

The man's shadow grew smaller, his voice louder. He had to be inches away. I reached into the side pocket of my bag. The timing needed to be perfect.

Heels clicked on the concrete floor. "If you came to work for me instead of him, I could make it worth your while."

"I'm not interested in working for anyone," Poe said. "I'm telling you—"

"Tell me this," the man said. "Are you interested in being alive?"

I raised my stun gun and stepped around the corner. "Are you?"

The man's eyes went wide when I tagged him in the chest. He hit the ground like a full sack of groceries, his limbs akimbo, still twitching. A wet spot spread across the front of his pants.

I looked up at Poe, who exhaled in relief. He had a fat lip and a trickle of blood coming from the corner of his mouth, and his left wrist was handcuffed to a doorknob.

"What happened?" I asked.

"I ported into the worst possible place. The guy was on me in seconds. He's the only one I saw, but I'm pretty sure he was waiting for backup."

"I hit the backup in the head with a stool. He shouldn't be a problem."

"That's my girl." Poe used his bloody right hand to gesture to his left. "I'm going to need a little help. Our friend with the bladder control problem made damn sure I wasn't going to get close enough to a veil to port out of here."

I checked the guy for the key to the cuffs, found it, and set Poe free.

"Do I want to know how you know what a handcuff key looks like?" he asked.

"Nope."

"Let's move." Poe slipped his knife out of his boot and I followed him into a long, wide room with a chill factor worthy of iceberg storage. Shelves lined the walls from floor to ceiling.

Poe scanned the room, muttering under his breath. "NT27. NT27. NT27—here."

The labeled shelf held a clock made of solid glass, with no internal hardware, but wildly spinning hands. An astrological chart beside it displayed lit, moving stars. A flat jewelry box held rings in different sizes. Some of them glowed.

"There." Poe pointed with the knife. "To the far left."

A small wooden chest stood open, revealing a pocket watch nestled in black velvet. It was the size of a half-dollar, the metal shiny, but not reflective. I picked it up. It was warm rather than cold. The gears on the back were exposed, but that was the only remarkable feature.

"I am not impressed. At all."

"You don't have to be." Poe tilted his head toward the open door. "Let's go."

"What about the other stuff?" I pointed to the rings and moving star chart. "We can't leave it here."

"What you're holding was handmade by Nikola Tesla. Thanks to his skills, it's more than a pocket watch—"

"Obviously."

"And," Poe continued, "worth more than everything in this room combined. Take it, and hurry, or you're going to end up fighting your way out of here."

I tucked the watch into my purse, and then I froze. Footsteps. More than one set.

"Too late." I looked at Poe and then handed him my bag. "Leave. Go while you can. I'll find a way to get out."

"Shut up." He grabbed my hand, pulling me away from the door to the storage room. He stopped and seemed to weigh his options. Before I could ask him what he was considering, he wrapped his arms around my waist and took a step back.

Time stopped.

Aching pressure closed around my heart and tightened like a fist. My lungs couldn't take in oxygen; blood didn't circulate through my veins. I was colder than I'd ever been, and then hotter. Pressure built up in my ears, like I was traveling over a high mountain or descending too fast while scuba diving.

Poe jerked me to one side and my feet were on solid ground again. All the pressure disappeared, but my head was still spinning.

I leaned over and retched.

"Hallie?" The timbre and tone of Poe's voice resonated as if he were speaking inside my head. I opened my eyes and saw distinct variations of color in his irises. "Are you okay?"

"What . . . the hell . . . was that?"

If he answered, I didn't hear him, because I was throwing up again.

Poe's hand was on my back. "Tell me you're okay."

"If barfing in bushes equals okay, then I am *super*."

He gathered my fake blue hair to hold it away from my face. I ripped the wig off and threw it down on the ground. I cupped my hands over my ears to stop the ringing before moving them to my eyes. They wouldn't stop tearing. I sat and put my head between my knees. A few minutes later, my hearing and vision returned to normal, and my stomach ceased the Tilt-a-Whirl. I was down to dry heaves now.

"What just happened?" I stood up slowly and faced Poe.

"I teleported you."

"But you can't teleport anyone. That's why I take cabs. You could've broken the whole of science. Or, you know, *me*."

"I didn't have a choice," he said, smoothing back my real hair. "Besides, we only moved a few miles, so I knew it would be fast."

I jerked away from him. "Don't ever, ever do that again."

"So next time, you want me to leave you to the mercy of men with guns?"

"Please do." I answered, and then promptly vomited again. Good thing our sexual attraction had played out, or I'd be embarrassed *and* pissed off. Once my stomach had calmed down, I straightened up. "Where are we? Is this Lafayette Cemetery?"

"Yes, but don't worry. No one else is here."

"Except for the dead people. And what if a cop shows up?" After-hours entry was punishable by law, and I didn't think Dad would be too happy if I got busted puking in a graveyard after hours. Oh, no, Officer, I haven't been drinking. It was *teleportation*.

The effects were wearing off, but I still felt weak enough to wonder if there had been some kind of permanent damage. I followed Poe down the broken sidewalk in the dark. As we approached the front gate of the cemetery, the late shift of waiters from Commander's Palace crowded onto the sidewalk across the street, laughing and teasing, not worried at all about keeping quiet or staying hidden.

"Get us out of here before someone sees us," I said. Poe held out his hand and I took a step back. "I will only accept a cab or piggyback ride. No more whirlwinds through the space time continuum."

"It's a couple of blocks to your house. If you want to walk the rest of the way, will you at least let me help you?"

"Help, please." I took the proffered arm, and we turned around.

And stopped dead.

A long trail of black-clad mourners snaked around the edge of the cemetery path. A solid mix of brass and percussion filled the air with the "Dead Man Blues," and church bells pealed. The casket passed by, followed by a second line of mourners with parasols and handkerchiefs, stepping in time to the music.

A jazz funeral, in the middle of the night, yet somehow in the middle of the day.

Completely out of place.

Completely out of time.

Chapter 2
Dune, November, Ivy Springs

"The Infinityglass is what?"

Liam Ballard, head of the Hourglass, and my boss, regarded me from across his desk with a cautious expression. "Human."

I sat back and let the notion settle in as I felt my eyes glaze over.

"Dune? Are you okay?" Liam asked.

I shook my head.

The Infinityglass was the freaking holy grail of time and believed to contain ultimate power over the space time continuum, among other things.

I'd been obsessed with it since I was a kid, heard endless stories about it from my dad, and imagined the Indiana Jones–type quest I'd eventually go on to find it.

Except that wasn't going to happen now, because *it* was *human*.

"Please tell me what you know." I leaned forward and gripped the edge of Liam's desk.

"I did some research." He tapped his fingers on a yellow legal pad full of chicken scratch. "Made a few phone calls. Got a few back. Went to the hospital to see Poe Sharpe."

"Poe. What does he have to do with it?"

Liam hesitated. Did some more finger tapping. Met my eyes. "Quite a bit."

"You're looking at me like you think my head's going to fly off and spin around the room." My forced laugh hung uncomfortably in the air. "Poe's not the Infinityglass, is he?"

"No. But you losing your head is a distinct possibility."

"Nothing can be crazier than the Infinityglass being . . . human." The word didn't even sit right on my tongue.

"When Poe came to us in October and gave us the ultimatum from Teague to find Jack Landers, I believed the order came from Chronos." Teague was the head of Chronos, otherwise known as the bad guys. Poe was her number-one henchman. Jack Landers was a world of trouble, who used to be second-in-command at the Hourglass. "I didn't even question it."

"Why would you?" I asked.

"Because I'm a scientist, and scientists are supposed to ask questions." Liam rubbed his temples. "Instead, I assumed everything was as it had been when I left—that Teague was in charge—and that the Chronos operations were still based in Memphis."

"But things have changed?"

"Ignoring something doesn't make it go away, and things evolve, whether you pay attention or not." Liam picked up a pen and started drawing on his legal pad, circling certain words over and over again. "Teague isn't in charge, and Chronos is no longer based in Memphis. Not only that, Chronos isn't our enemy."

"After everything Poe and Teague did—"

"Teague was acting in her *own* interests. Poe was duped into carrying out orders issued by her, but he believed he was working for the real organization."

"If Teague isn't in charge of Chronos, who is?"

"Paul Girard. Teague's estranged husband."

"That doesn't seem like that big of a deal. What am I missing?"

"It's not one thing; it's the combination of many. Lily's the one who made me realize the Infinityglass is human." Lily Garcia, the newest member of the Hourglass, had a supernatural ability to find anything or anyone. "She searched for an object and found nothing. Then she looked for a person and got an address."

I actually put my hands on top of my head, wondering if its removal would be a relief at this point. "You know where the Infinityglass is."

Liam nodded. "Who it is, too."

"A him or a her?"

"A her."

"Human . . . how?" I couldn't wrap my mind around it. "Is she immortal?"

"She's seventeen."

"But the lore—not that it's lore anymore—has been around forever. How can she be so young?"

"There's an explanation, and I'm certain it's as elusive as everything else about the Infinityglass."

"She's not safe." It hit me that we were talking about a human. A life. More than a legend.

Liam rubbed his temples again. "She is for the moment, but probably not for long."

The questions were coming too fast for me to keep up with my own brain. "Does she know what she is? Where is she?"

"I don't know if she knows, and she's in New Orleans, at the Girard's home address."

"The Girard's home address. *Teague's* home address?" My stomach pitched as I connected the dots. "Teague has the Infinityglass. She's already beaten us to her."

"By about seventeen years. I have reason to believe the Infinityglass is Teague Girard's daughter."

Holy hell.

"What I need to know now is"—Liam leaned forward and nailed me with a long stare—"are you going with me to find her?"

If I was going to get the Infinityglass, I was going to need to make some changes.

Nate's mouth hung open so wide I could see his wisdom teeth. "You're going to do what?"

"Cut them off." I dropped the clippers and the scissors on the kitchen counter with a clatter.

"Why? Dreads are sexy," Lily said, earning a side glance from Kaleb. After he growled, she reached across the kitchen table to run her hand through his hair. He was growing it out after a skull trim. "But I like short better."

"Maybe you should just leave it long, Dune," Kaleb said to me, before grabbing her arm and putting his lips to her wrist.

I didn't bother responding. Kaleb was too busy focusing on Lily and whatever he was doing to make her breath catch. Since they'd gotten together, they never stopped touching, and they were always at our place. The way they connected made me miss something I'd never had.

"It's time for a change. Don't you think?" I turned to Nate now, although if I were going to ask for style advice, his would be the last I'd take. His perpetually neon streak of hair was some-where between pink and orange this week. "Besides, it's only hair."

"It's not just hair," Nate argued. "It's your trademark."

"It's your excuse to call me Chewbacca."

"I'll just call you Bald Chewbacca now."

"You're a good friend."

"Fine." Nate picked up the scissors and snapped them open and closed. A little too joyfully and a little too quickly. "If this is going to happen, do I get to do the honors?"

I preferred a gentle touch, but Lily and Kaleb had disap-peared. Again.

"I guess so. Do *not* shoot for speed, Nate." Nate had the ability to speed up or slow down his movements. "Aim for accuracy."

Nate tapped the back of a chair and grinned.

I sat down and shut my eyes.

The bathroom mirror was steamy, so I used my ability to turn the gas to liquid. Condensation rolled down the glass in rivulets.

I stared at the image that remained, trying to adjust. My sideburns kept me from feeling like a plucked chicken, but the lack of hair was going to take some getting used to. I pulled on a pair of worn jeans and went back to the kitchen. Nate had bundled up the remains of my dreads and tied them in a pink ribbon.

The smart-ass presented it to me like it was some kind of bouquet. "I didn't know if you wanted to have a burial."

I took a long look at six years' worth of hair, and then threw it in the trash.

Nate leaned back against the wall, studying the change. "This is pretty serious."

"It was time for a change." Time to grow up.

"Why?" He pushed off the wall with one foot and started pacing. "We've known each other for how many years? Five, at least? The Dune I know is laidback, dependable. He makes logical, balanced decisions, applies all the facts, weighs the pros and cons. This feels impulsive, and you aren't impulsive."

"I've been thinking about cutting them off for a while." That wasn't a lie. I'd even been letting them grow out, which was the only reason I wasn't totally bald.

"The hair isn't the only issue. Something's up. Is this about getting a girlfriend or some stupid crap like that?"

"No," I protested, even though my luck with the ladies had been off. The way the Hourglass employees were pairing up reminded me of Noah's ark. I didn't want to cruise into the sunset with Nate.

"You started going to the gym a couple of months ago. You just bought new clothes." He pointed to the bags on the counter.

"Some of my Samoan cousins lean toward the Rock. Others, not as much. I know which way I want to go." The gym had been about fear of turning fat. "But you're right. Buying the clothes was intentional."

"Because?"

"I'm going on a job."

Nate's eyes narrowed. "What kind of job requires a dude makeover?"

"It's not a makeover. It's an upgrade. I can't be a kid forever." I didn't want to be. "Professionals don't wear T-shirts that say, 'Bazinga.'"

The front door burst open. The gust of cold air had me covering my head with my hands. When I saw Emerson, I covered my nipples instead.

Because I was a dork.

"Whoa, Nelly!" Emerson stopped so fast Michael almost ran over her. She dropped the grocery bags she held on the kitchen table and stared at me with a frightening kind of glee on her face. "*Dune.* You're scary. And hot. Scary hot. Who knew?"

Michael took a step back and fanned himself. "I have the vapors."

"I like it." Em approached me the way a cat might approach a still-wriggling puffer fish, from multiple angles and with a cautious eye. "But where's your shirt?"

"He got some new ones. Because he's a grown-up." Nate's annoying singsongy tone set my teeth on edge.

"Um. Dune?" Em bit her lower lip. "I know what nipples look like."

I sighed, lowered my hands, and decided I really needed to get out more.

Nate threw me one of the button-ups I'd found on sale at the mall, along with a vest I'd snagged at the thrift shop. I caught them right before they hit me in the face.

The door opened again, allowing another blast of cold air. Ava. She stopped and stared at my head. "Where are your dreads?"

I pointed to the trash can.

"I think I like it." She walked past me with raised eyebrows and tucked herself into a corner, taking on her usual observer role.

"Okay. Try the bowler on first," Em urged, picking up a hat and shoving it at me. "This is going to be yummy."

"We need to see the shirts, too," Michael said, smiling. That was only another example of why he and Emerson fit together the way they did. Even with all the trouble we'd seen lately, he'd never smiled like that before her.

"It must be nice to be so secure in your relationship," I said to him, smoothing out the now-crumpled bowler hat.

"She loves me," he answered simply.

"I love him." Em smiled.

"Listen," I said, spinning the hat on my finger. "If you people think I'm going to play dress-up—"

"I want a montage." Em reached in one of the grocery bags and pulled out a bag of clementines. She took a couple out and threw one to Ava, then tossed the rest of the package to Michael, who caught it neatly before stowing it in the crisper drawer of the fridge.

"Montage?" I asked.

"Yeah, like those cheesy eighties movies, where the girl— or guy—tries on all kinds of new clothes and twirls around in front of a full-length mirror and a crowd of friends. To make sure everything works and that her butt doesn't look too big."

"Or his butt, right?" I asked. Em was the perfect ray of sarcastic sunshine.

"Right." She smiled. "So we'll be right here waiting for you to montage. I'll try to find some good music. Maybe Pat Benatar or Prince or the Go-Go's. I think you have the beat, Dune."

Ava tossed me a plaid ivy cap. "Try that one, too, or I might steal it."

I caught it easily. "One thing. I'll try on one thing with one hat, just to make sure—"

"That your butt doesn't look big. We know." Em made a shoo-ing motion. "Try to enter at the beginning of the chorus. Bonus if you put a flower between your teeth."

Michael followed me back to my room with Nate on his heels. "What's with the wardrobe change?"

"Nothing." I undid the top three buttons on the white shirt, removed the tags, and pulled it over my head. The sensation of the cloth against my now bare neck gave me the willies.

"How dense do you think I am?" Michael asked. "It's more than clothes. You cut off your *hair.*"

Nate dropped into my desk chair. "We're calling him Bald Chewbacca now."

"I am not bald." I threw the crumpled tags at his head. "It's at least half an inch long."

"I'm not changing your nickname." Nate jerked his head in Michael's direction, and then leaned back on two chair legs. "Either you tell him about the job or I will. But I'm guessing he already knows."

"Maybe." Michael watched as I took a pin-striped vest out of my closet. "But I have no problem waiting right here until you give me your take on it, Dune."

"You want my opinion on things?" I slipped my arms into the

vest. "I've got time to kill. Maybe you'd like to hear my theories on the existence of the chupacabra instead?"

Neither one of them moved.

"What about my thoughts on the dangers of *Warcraft* possibly overtaking *Star Wars* as *the* franchise gold mine?"

"Lies!" Nate yelled.

I grinned. I knew how to get him distracted.

"Tell us about the job, Dune." Michael leaned back against my wall and crossed his arms over his chest.

"Fine." I blew out a sigh. "Liam called me into his office last week. The Infinityglass is a person."

"What?" Nate sucked wind and almost fell out of his chair. "You knew this for a *week* and you didn't tell me?"

"I wanted to, trust me. But Liam wanted it kept quiet."

Michael didn't react at all, which confirmed he'd already been privy to the information. Not surprising. Liam had been grooming him to take over the Hourglass for a while, so he usually knew more than the rest of us.

I looked Michael in the eye. "I still don't understand why Liam wanted me for the job instead of you."

"You know more about the Infinityglass than anyone, even Liam," Michael pointed out. "You're perfect for this."

"Maybe, but I tend to fly under the radar. This is a little high profile for me."

"Hello? The Infinityglass is a person? How?" Nate waved his arms over his head. "Can we talk about that part?"

I gave him the short version of Liam's long explanation. "The Infinityglass has to be activated—"

"Like the Wonder Twins?" Nate mimicked bumping two rings together, making a *kapow* sound when he pulled his fists away from each other.

His levity disappeared when I stared at him.

"Sorry. Please proceed."

"We don't know what causes the activation, but something kicks the gene into gear," I explained.

Michael spoke up, more confirmation that Liam had completely filled him in. "While we all activated in puberty, it takes more than that to get the Infinityglass going, and the connection doesn't always happen. That's why the 'sightings' are so limited."

"But we have Lily," I said, "and she nailed down a location. The girl lives in New Orleans, and she happens to be Teague's daughter."

"Teague's daughter? The Infinityglass is human, and she's Teague's daughter. Poor kid, to have *that* for a parent." Nate dropped the chair back to all four legs with a thud. "I need a few years to take this in."

"You can't have years. Liam and I are going to Louisiana in five days."

"You're going to help her. I can get on board with that." Nate nodded thoughtfully. "But if Teague's her mom, how are you going to get to her?"

"Teague isn't involved in her life. She lives with her dad, and he has a badass reputation. Sort of a . . . mobster."

"A mobster who's the true head of Chronos," Michael added.

"So you're going to New Orleans to meet a gangster and his . . . legendary daughter, and this requires short hair and a beefcake, hipster vibe?" Nate didn't sound convinced.

"It requires that I look responsible. This guy has to take me seriously, and his daughter needs all the help she can get. And I'm not a hipster."

"Hipstercrite, maybe. Hold on a second." Nate held up a hand. "Why was Teague looking for the Infinityglass if the Infinityglass is her daughter? Surely she knows?"

"Teague wasn't looking for the Infinityglass. She was looking for *Jack*, who was looking for the Infinityglass," Michael explained. "Teague was either trying to keep Jack away from the truth, or there was something else she wanted on the Skroll."

"It sounds like Teague is protecting her daughter." Nate leaned back on two chair legs again. "Why are you going to New Orleans? Why not just make a phone call?"

"Because every source tells us that Teague isn't to be trusted, including her husband. Liam talked to him. He wants us to come to NOLA as much as we want to go. I might be staying." I ran my hand over my head. "Hence the hairdo."

A sudden blast of music made us all jump, and the bass thumped hard enough to bounce a couple of pencils off my desk.

Grateful for the interruption, I asked, "Is that . . . ?"

"New Kids on the Block," Nate said, already dancing in his chair.

I looked at Michael. "Em's going to make me spin around, isn't she?"

"Oh no, my man." Michael clapped me on the shoulder. "She's going to make you *twirl*."

Five days later, Liam and I were in his truck, heading for the Nashville airport.

The blasting heat inside the cab made the skin on my face tighten. An early winter had settled into middle Tennessee with a passion. Seventy-five degrees on Halloween, twenty-nine the next day, and it hadn't warmed up much since.

"Not to mess with your creaky old-man bones," I said, "but I'm already a sweat puddle."

Liam smiled and turned the heat down. "You don't need to worry."

"I'm not worried, just hot." I might have believed it myself if my voice hadn't cracked in the middle of the sentence. "Are you sure about this?"

"I am."

As he merged onto I-65 north, I fidgeted with the seat belt, pulling it above and below my shoulder to find a comfortable position. Finally, I just sat on my hands to keep them still. I was too broad in the shoulders to get truly comfortable, anyway.

Liam checked his rearview mirror. "I know switching the Infinityglass paradigm from object to human has been difficult."

"What hasn't been difficult this year?"

The dead had come back to life. Time had been rewritten.

The space time continuum had been damaged. Anyone with the basic time gene could see ripples; imprints of people from the past, which had turned into entire scenes, streets full of people, even buildings. These rips were getting worse. Their latest evolution had trapped Michael and Em inside one, and they'd barely escaped.

Liam's answering smile was more of a grimace. "Too true. There is one thing we haven't discussed, and it should've had priority. Is it going to be difficult for you to be near so much water?"

I stared out the window and thought about the question. Frost covered fields like powdered sugar as we passed everything from mansions to tiny farmhouses. Livestock stood in huddles to keep warm, their breaths rising into the air. Half-frozen ponds waited for spring.

Harmless, still water.

Besides the Harpeth, I hadn't been near a river in months, and now I was heading for New Orleans and its neighbors, the Mississippi, Lake Pontchartrain, and the Gulf of Mexico.

"I think it's going to be okay." I hoped it was. "But don't expect me to spend a lot of time by the water."

Liam stared straight ahead, his eyebrows puckered in

concentration. "I won't leave you in a circumstance you aren't comfortable with. That's a promise."

"I know that." I adjusted the seat belt again, and tried to change the subject. "What I'm not comfortable with is you leaving Ivy Springs. Grace needs you."

Liam's wife had just come out of a nine-month-long coma.

"Hallie Girard needs us, too. I'll only be away for a day. Two, max."

All I knew about Hallie was that she was seventeen, and for some reason, really isolated. I'd done more than one Internet search on her. She didn't have any social media profiles. I wondered if being the Infinityglass had affected her life in some horrible way.

"What's her dad going to think when you offer up a tech geek to him?"

"Luckily, he and I have a history, even if it's only because we met through Teague. Her betrayal didn't surprise him. She abandoned her family long ago. It's heartbreaking, honestly, especially for the daughter." Liam switched lanes. "As far as the Infinityglass, he knew about it, but believed the same thing we did. That it was an object."

"How did he take it when you told him it was his daughter?" I asked.

"Hard. But he believed me."

I wondered what being an all-powerful, mythical "thing" could do to a girl. I wondered if she had symptoms.

Liam exited for the airport, heading for short-term parking. After he picked a spot and killed the engine, I got out and removed our suitcases from the back of the truck.

"If it doesn't work, if you have any qualms, you come back home with me," Liam said. "Deal?"

I looked up at the Nashville International Airport and answered the only way I could.

"Deal."

Dune, Mid-November, New Orleans

There were already Christmas decorations up in the airport.

We left baggage claim and waited on the sidewalk for a taxi. Tourists were everywhere. Groups of tipsy college kids who'd gotten an early start on Bourbon Street, married couples ready for a getaway weekend, and us.

I tried to take in as much of the city as I could on the cab ride, but nerves and the smell of the water kept my gut twisted. Ivy Springs had its share of history spread out over a lot of mileage, but the Garden District's history was dense and compact.

Dormers and gables, porches and columns, all layered with intricate detail. Everything was white or pastel, except for the bark of the massive oaks and the leaves on their branches. The tree roots grew so large that the sidewalk broke into pieces above them.

Among all that beauty, the Girard house was best described as nouveau riche penitentiary.

A big guy with a holstered firearm buzzed us through the gate and inside the front door. The *air* smelled like money. After a few seconds, we were led to Paul Girard's "library."

It was grandiose, an obnoxious kind of new South. Everything was shiny, or new and dulled down to look old. I was used to Liam's home office, which was nice enough, but dusty and full of books and his personal collection of hourglasses. Liam's office looked like he worked in it. Paul Girard's library looked like he posed in it.

"Come in." Girard stood. He was your basic slick-haired, shifty-eyed, moneyed gangster, with excellent taste in suits.

After introductions, Girard asked about our flight and general well-being, but the chitchat didn't last long. Liam sat down, and so did I, balancing on the edge of a masculine couch.

"You're the guy who's supposed to help my daughter?" Girard sounded doubtful.

"Yes, sir." I nodded.

He looked me over, summed me up. "Try to relax."

I slid back on the seat. It was the best I could manage.

Girard continued the stare-down. "Try to relax *more*."

I put one arm on the back of the couch and smiled. Felt my lips wobble. Wanted to go home really, really, desperately.

Liam took pity on my inner introvert. "Dune has been with the Hourglass for several years. I've told you about his work history, so you know he's reliable. He also happens to have more knowledge about the Infinityglass than anyone, even myself."

"Knowledge. Great." Girard tilted his head to the side, regarding me. "Does he talk?"

"He . . . yes." I'd never seen Liam falter before.

"I do." I moved back to the edge of the couch. "Talk, I mean."

When Girard shifted, I saw the gun holster under his jacket. Everyone in this house was armed. "The Infinityglass. What do you know?"

This was my chance. "Horologists name it as one of the biggest finds in the field, at least the ones who cop to its being real."

"I'm certain my daughter is real."

I made a sound somewhere between a gulp and a laugh. "Well, horologists believe it's an object, not a human. I should explain what horo—"

"I know what horology is. Liam started out doing all your talking for you. Do horologists do all your thinking for you? What makes *you* believe it's a human?"

I looked at Liam, and he handed over the briefcase I'd felt too self-conscious to carry. I flipped the latches and pushed it toward Girard. "That's my personal external drive. It holds every shred of evidence ever collected on the Infinityglass, a couple of hundred years' worth, and includes new information that was recently discovered on a Skroll."

"A scroll?"

"Not the old-school kind. A digital storage device, kind of like a tablet on steroids, with holograms." This specific Skroll held information about the Infinityglass, and had changed hands too many times to count. "The Hourglass stole the Skroll from your wife. She never managed to get it open. I did."

It had taken me two weeks to crack it.

"Do you still have it?" Girard asked.

"No. We gave it back to your wife. I have everything that was on it. And I left it altered. Now it's missing some vital documents." Taking information off the Skroll had been a gamble, and one that could have cost lives. From where I sat now, the risk had been worth it. "The information on this Skroll is the key to the Infinity-glass. I've read through everything I can, and I'm in the process of translating the rest. There's centuries of information to cover."

"You're here because a man I trusted deeply believed in you." He looked at Liam. "All I'm interested in is what being the Infinity-glass means to my daughter."

Liam gestured to me. "That's why I brought you Dune."

I nodded. "Finding out is my goal, sir, and I'm one hundred percent committed to it."

"If you work for the Hourglass, you have an ability. What is it?"

I swallowed, hard. "I can control water. The tides. Moon phases—that's how it's connects with the time gene. It's not something I mess with very often. Too hard to control."

"Yet you come to New Orleans. 'Water, water everywhere, nor any drop to drink.'" The man had been in my presence for all of five minutes, and had already zeroed in on one of my biggest fears and quoted "The Rime of the Ancient Mariner" in the process. "How are you going to handle the mighty Mississippi so close by?"

"I don't plan on spending much time by the river. Or lake. Or the ocean. Nothing volatile. If working for you requires me to do so . . . I'll find a way around it."

I didn't look at Liam. He knew what a job involving that much water would do to me. The last job I'd been on for the Hourglass that involved my ability had been the previous summer. A tiny country stream had required a reroute from a floodplain. I'd shaped the water as I controlled it long enough to move it to the new trench that had been dug. Then Nate and I had helped fill the now-dry section of creek bed with clay mud.

I'd acted like it was simple, no problem at all, but I'd seen a dead fish on the grass, a result of my shoddy navigation, and I'd had to fight off panic.

"I don't foresee a circumstance in which your being on the water would be necessary. Unless you can't handle the pool in the back."

"That's not a problem."

Girard sat back in his seat. "Tell me what you know about my business."

I gave him the short version because I didn't know how to

approach the long one. "You deal in rare antiquities. People with time-related abilities assist."

"Succinct. Diplomatic. Nice." Girard crossed his ankle over one knee. "The Hourglass has a very high bar when it comes to morality. I acquire antiquities under certain furtive circumstances. If you're going to come to work for me, you are, indeed, going to work for *me*. Jobs that could cause the wrong sorts of people to ask questions. Are you prepared to answer them?"

I didn't know if the wrong sorts of people were the good guys or the bad. Paul Girard had no time-related ability, but businessmen like him were genius judges of human nature. Uncertainty wouldn't do in this situation.

"I'm prepared."

"Good. Ideally, I can keep you out of that end, since your main purpose is helping my daughter. But if it becomes part of your cover, so be it. I don't want Hallie to know what you're really doing here." He stared at me and I nodded, confirming I was totally on board. "I told her I was planning to hire new security. We'll let her believe you're part of her new detail."

"I don't—I have no idea how to be a bodyguard. I don't even know how to fake it."

"It doesn't matter. I rarely have anyone on her in the house. She'll be really, really pissed off, and my daughter, pissed off . . ." He looked at me like he felt sorry for me.

"Does she have any idea she's the Infinityglass?" Liam asked.

"Her ability is transmutation. I don't believe she knows she's the Infinityglass."

Liam's frown went wrinkle deep. "Do you plan on telling her?"

"That depends." Girard asked, focusing on me, "Do you have answers for her?"

"I need to observe her for a little while. I need time to try to reconcile the differences between what I thought the Infinityglass was and what it truly is and to finish translating and studying all the information on the Skroll."

"Then we'll wait until you know something solid. I don't want to scare her with half-truths." He stood, and so did Liam and I. "If Liam says you're my best option, I'll believe him, because I have every reason to believe in the Hourglass. I know what you stand for and what you do. But if you prove him or me wrong . . ."

Girard left the threat unspoken.

And somehow that was scarier than if he'd said it aloud.

Chapter 3

Hallie, Mid-November

After the pawnshop job, I told my dad I'd be taking a paid vacation.

I did my normal Rapunzel-in-the-tower thing, with nothing to break it up except dance class three times a week, and I didn't even leave the house for that. Dad had converted a detached building on our property into my very own studio and hired a private teacher. Things were lonely. Boring.

But not normal.

Something changed the night Poe and I did the job at Skeevy's. It all started with the jazz funeral in the graveyard.

I'd known the timing was off. No one would be having a funeral at night, and anyway, sunlight surrounded the mourners. The group had entered from the front gate of the cemetery, going right past the waiters and waitresses from Commander's Palace, but none of the waitstaff had noticed. New Orleans ladies were known for good hats, but the shoes and outfits were wrong. Too many prints. Boxy purses and heels.

Then, the next day from my bedroom window, I saw men putting the finishing touches on the Saint Charles Avenue line, which had already existed for almost two hundred years. Gone were the Mardi Gras beads that usually hung from the electric wires and gone was the grass that lined either side of the rails. I saw freshly turned dirt, and the southern live oaks that lined the street were way smaller than they were supposed to be. The streetcars were new and shiny, standing like soldiers awaiting their chance to serve the city.

The next day, from the kitchen, I'd watched a solid stream of ladies and gentlemen traveling by horse and carriage, going visiting.

I knew what I was seeing, but I didn't know why.

Years ago, my mom had found a set of twins in the foster care system. She'd hooked them up with a family far out in the bayou. A family that was well compensated and therefore didn't mind when the twins accidentally shorted out electrical appliances. A family that wasn't privy to the fact that Amelia and Zooey were time travelers.

Countless things have been lost throughout time. The *Titanic* sank with untold riches on board. The Amber Room disappeared during World War II. Some of the biggest art heists of all time had yet to yield their spoils. That was how time travelers were useful to Chronos.

When Hemingway's first wife, Hadley, walked away from a suitcase full of his manuscripts at Paris Lyon to buy a bottle of water, Amelia and Zooey popped in. The suitcase was lost to history, but the manuscripts showed up in New Orleans.

A priceless Degas was thought to be lost in a fire, but miraculously appeared in the collection of a certain family that lived on Esplanade.

And so on and so forth.

A time-travel side effect was that Amelia and Zooey saw ripples all the time. Once I made the mistake of telling them I thought it was cool. They started describing them whenever we were together just to get on my nerves. Now people like me, who shouldn't be able to see rips, could.

The space time continuum was screwed.

The jazz funeral I'd seen progressing toward Lafayette Cemetery was a rip, just like everything else I'd seen from my window. I was crossing the courtyard to go to dance class the first time I saw a rip face-to-face.

She sat perched on a bench in the courtyard, holding a porcelain doll in her tiny hands. It resembled her, with delicate, perfectly even features, and even wore a similar dress, adorned with an abundance of lace. Two guys from Dad's security detail were standing outside, too. They didn't see her.

When I walked past, she took no notice, just continued to play with her tiny doppelganger, singing a lullaby in French. Nowhere close to a ghostly specter, she was as solid as the stone patio beneath my feet. I ignored her. I had other things to think about.

Rips like her weren't my only problem.

✾

As usual, dance was my release. I spent a good two hours pretending everything was normal.

"The fund-raiser showcase for Southern Rep is in March," Gina, who was my favorite pointe teacher, said at the end of the session. "You're ready to perform. You barely broke a sweat today."

"Maybe I'm just dehydrated."

"You're strong. You've always been able to dance circles around me, but I bet you could cover all the geometric shapes now."

"You know what they say. Once you hit twenty-one, everything starts going downhill." I stuck my tongue out at her and escaped into the dressing room before she could push me any further.

She knew I wouldn't participate in the showcase. All of my teachers had mentioned it, and all of them had been blown off. My dad was too cautious to put me on display.

I untied the ribbons of my pointe shoes and pulled my feet out, preparing to remove layers of lamb's wool and cotton to see how bad the damage was. I anticipated bloody toes, so I grabbed medical tape and scissors.

I'd ended up dancing because of an injury. Four surgeries and a pin in my shinbone—because I'd healed too fast from a gunshot wound. The doctor ignored the healing rate, probably paid off by my mother, and insisted that I do something physical beyond my three-times-a-week physical therapy. Dance was the answer. A few forced years at a combination tap, jazz, and ballet class as a child had taught me the basics, but rather than send me to a class out in the big bad world post accident, Dad had converted a building on our property and hired private teachers. My jail of a home life might have been all lock-down penitentiary, but at least my prison had a dance studio.

Dancing in the showcase wasn't my dream, and if I had to put up a fuss, the fuss wouldn't be for that. Newcomb, Tulane's School of Liberal Arts, on the other hand, had a dance major. Whatever I decided to do with my life wouldn't be easy. If I wanted out of the Chronos prison my father had built for me, I'd be in for a fight.

I removed the wrapping from my toes and geared myself up for the damage.

There was nothing there. My toes were whole and perfect, not a scab or a scrape to be seen.

"What the hell?" I stared at the stained wool in my hands and sorted through all the layers before doing the same with the cotton. I'd always healed fast.

But never this fast.

It was in line with everything else that had been wrong lately. I wanted to talk to Poe, and I'd texted, but he wasn't answering.

I pushed up off the floor and headed for the shower, stripping my arms out of my leotard before I shut the door.

I couldn't sleep. Or eat. I didn't need to. My vision had sharpened. The simplest of sounds echoed inside my brain like monosyllabic earworms. When I practiced changing my body, I could hold shapes without tiring. At all. I'd even been able to manipulate my vocal cords.

I stared at my God-given body in the full-length mirror. Hours of dance kept me thin, but I'd finally gotten past the awkward side of it, thanks to muscle tone. Smooth, fair skin, even though there should've been scars on my shoulder and my leg. Dark brown hair and hazel eyes, like my mother.

I turned away from the mirror and stepped into the shower.

When I got out, I had a new text. Dad, requesting an audience.

I avoided looking at the bench as I crossed the courtyard. No little girl, but the lullaby still hung in the air, floating on the cold autumn wind.

The Chronos offices occupied a full square block in the Central Business District, just off Canal, in a building designated for Girard Industries. Heavy security discouraged most visitors, and if anyone managed to get through, two floors of apparent telemarketers would've bored them away. Most days, my dad worked from that building. But today, I'd been called to his home office.

I liked to call it the throne room. He didn't like it at all.

"Poe is *where?*"

"Tennessee." Dad wore his usual poker face. "ICU at the Vanderbilt University Medical Center. He was hurt, badly, but is expected to recover."

"How—"

"I don't know how, Hallie. Just that he had a terrible knife injury and almost bled to death. But he didn't."

I blew out a deep breath. Dad's words rolled through my brain like the crawler at the bottom of a news broadcast.

"When's he coming back to New Orleans?" I asked.

Dad's eyes closed briefly, and he pinched the bridge of his nose between his thumb and index finger.

"Dad?"

"No idea." He dropped his hand. "But if I let him come back, things are going to change."

If. I wanted to let loose, like Godzilla on an unsuspecting city, but people crossed oceans to avoid Paul Girard's anger. Not a good idea to cause more if I wanted to get Poe back.

"No one else has the same skill he does," I said, trying to reason. "Are you really willing to let him walk?"

"Possibly, yes."

"Can we talk about *why*?"

My father went to the mahogany liquor cabinet, took a few ice cubes from the ice bucket, and dropped them into a glass. He poured a glass half full of amber-colored liquid. It was only on the rocks because lunchtime hadn't rolled around yet. After that, it was straight-up.

"Poe's loyalties have come into question."

"Who would he be loyal to besides us?"

Dad set his glass down firmly and wiped his mouth with his thumb. His hands went to his hips, pushing back his suit jacket, exposing the lines of his holster.

"No," I said. "No way. Not Poe."

The cutting edge of betrayal overrode the feeling of dread *she* usually conjured up.

My mother.

"How did you find out?" I asked.

"She called. As a courtesy."

I could imagine how courteous that conversation had been.

Dad and I didn't talk about her, and only in business terms when we did. She'd done a bunk when I was ten, though she'd stayed at Chronos. I rarely went on jobs for her and had started to refuse them altogether, so a couple of years ago, she'd "made things easier for all of us" by choosing to operate out of her own office. She'd only made things easier for herself.

Teague Girard might be able to give up her family, but she'd sure as hell stick around for science.

"Why? Why would Poe do that?"

"I think you should sit down," Dad said.

My head came up sharply. *Weakness* wasn't in Paul Girard's vocabulary, yet he sounded unsure.

"You know I'm about business. Always have been." He filled

his glass a little higher than halfway this time. "That's why your mother pursued me, because of my connections and business sense."

Not because she loved him.

"She brought Chronos to me." He took a drink. "This much you know."

I nodded.

"Chronos had chosen to be esoteric instead of savvy, and she wanted to change that. Time is money, and things were going downhill. There are people with special time skills all over the world. I didn't know about those talents until your mother. Once I believed, I threw my backing behind Chronos. It didn't take me very long to see the benefits, so I got involved." He swirled the Maker's Mark whisky in his glass. "There were people who didn't agree with the way your mother wanted to handle things. One is the head of the Hourglass."

"The ones who do the squeaky clean jobs?"

"The perfectly legal ones, yes." He took another drink, a long one. "Your mother has recently been involved with them."

"If they're into legality, why would they hook up with her? Don't they know who she is?" *How* she is?

"I don't think they had a lot of choice in the matter."

Mom had sacrificed our familial relationship, and now she'd ditched our business one, too. She couldn't cut us out any more clearly if she'd used an X-Acto knife.

"And as far as Poe is concerned, I believe your mother persuaded him to help her instead of us."

The hits just kept coming.

"He wouldn't betray me like that." He couldn't have. He was my only friend.

"I hope not, Hallie, but I'm not sure what to expect from anyone anymore, and until I know exactly what your mother is up to, I'm going to hire extra security."

"Come on, Dad," I whined in protest. "What are you going to do, put a guard on every inside door?"

"Just yours."

I put my face in my hands to stifle the sound of my groan. "You can't—"

"I can. I'm making my final decision this afternoon." He set his jaw. "Whoever I choose will start tomorrow. Prepare yourself."

My phone rang just as I reached the top of the stairs.

I didn't want to answer, but I always did. I stopped in front of the window seat in the upper hallway that looked out over the street. "Hello, Mother."

"Good morning, Hallie."

"It's already afternoon." I wondered if she was in a different time zone. I strained to listen for background noises on her end of the line.

"Why must you always split hairs?"

"What do you want?" I dropped down onto the red velvet cushion and watched a dragonfly repeatedly crash into the window. I figured they'd all have taken to the swamps with the recent cold snap.

"You've usually hung up by this point in our conversations. What's stopping you today?"

Poe. The fact that my mother always had me on a hook. The endless pull between wanting her approval and wishing she didn't exist at all. It tore at me constantly, leaving my insides busted up and oozing. "I know you want something. Might as well find out what it is now."

"I wanted to talk to you."

"Please."

She sighed. "There's something you and Poe retrieved for your father. I need to know its location."

"Oh. That's why I rank a phone call."

"You rank a phone call because you're my daughter."

"Don't." I knew it was wrong to roll around in all my upper handedness, but damned if it didn't feel good. "You know my involvement ends after the jobs are done. I'm not privy to the location of things, and I seriously doubt Dad would leave whatever you're looking for lying around for some idiot to come across."

The implication that she was the idiot remained unspoken, but I rolled around and got dirty in it, too.

She paused. "It doesn't have to be this way between us."

I stared at the dragonfly, still bumping against the glass. You'd think it would've given up by now.

"Yes, it does. Maybe you should call Dad. Maybe he'll accidentally pick up, and you can try to weasel the answer out of him."

I knew she'd already tried. The Poe information had been offered up to try to grease the wheel, and when she hadn't gotten anything from Dad, she'd bounced to me. Good thing Dad and I could always see her coming.

"Don't hang up on me, Hallie." It was said in a definite "mother" tone.

"You almost sound like you're pulling the parent discipline card. And I *know* that didn't just happen." My grip on the phone was deathly. I breathed in through my nose, down to my stomach, like Gina taught me. When I exhaled through my mouth, I loosened my fingers. "Can we be done now?"

"Did you tell your father that you were seeing ripples?"

How did she know?

"I'm not a traveler," I said cautiously. "Why would I see rips?"

"You aren't the only one. So am I. It's impacting everyone with the time gene. Poe, too."

The mention of Poe sparked my anger, but I didn't show it. Giving her the satisfaction of knowing how much it bugged me would burn me from the inside out. I wanted to ask her where he was, but held back on that, too. It wasn't like I could trust her answer, anyway.

"I talked to Amelia and Zooey," she continued, and I could

swear I heard a tinge of smug. "They both tell me the usual rules don't apply anymore. They used to be able to talk to a rip when they saw one, singular. Now they see multiples, and the rips don't acknowledge them."

Someone was going to need to get on the horn and tell A. and Z. to keep their traps shut when it came to my mom.

"Thanks for the info." If she thought I was giving her anything in exchange, she'd cracked. "I'll take it under consideration."

"Seeing rips isn't all that's happening to you, is it, Hallie?"

So sly. Trepidation coiled in my gut. "What do you mean?"

She paused for a minute, and I could see her pacing as she considered what to say, looking out a window onto an unknown city.

"Your cells are regenerating faster and faster. All your faculties now operate at optimal performance. You're getting stronger every day."

I sniffed. "I hope it's after five wherever you are, because you sound like you're three sheets to the wind."

"You aren't sleeping. Your mouth can't keep up with your brain. I can help you, Hallie." Her voice was soft, but there was nothing gentle about it. "I'm your mother, and you can trust me."

I bit back a laugh.

"Say the word. All you have to do is say the word and I'll be there."

"Here's a word. Good-bye."

"Remember the bedtime stories?" she asked before I could hang up.

I stilled, my grip on the phone tightening again. She was persistent. I'd give her that.

"The ones I used to tell you about an object with abilities that couldn't be imagined. The Infinityglass had power that could change worlds. You used to believe in that power."

Our bedtime ritual had been my one constant when Mom lived with us. From the time I was a preschooler until I was ten, every night, I had my bath, a cup of chamomile tea, and story time with my mama. Then she left.

To this day, the smell of chamomile gave me a stomachache.

"Turns out it wasn't an object, Hallie. It was a person. You understand what I'm saying, don't you? You can feel it."

"I can't feel anything." I meant it, just not in the way she was referring to.

"When you decide you want to know the truth, I'm a phone call away."

"If I wanted the truth, Mother, I most certainly wouldn't get it from you."

I disconnected, and dropped the phone on the red velvet cushion.

Chapter 4

Dune

When the cab dropped me off in front of the Georgian Apartments, I asked the driver to double-check we were at the right address. A brown portico extended over the entryway, and deep green ivy covered the entire facade. I stepped onto the sidewalk, finally understanding how huge the southern live oaks were.

What I didn't understand was how a job as a faux security guard had scored me a place in a swank apartment building like this one.

The lobby was just as impressive, black-and-white-tiled floors, tasteful art, chandeliers that sparkled, and a doorman in a uniform. I walked past him to the manager's office and found a college-aged girl sitting behind a receptionist desk. "I'm Dune Ta'ala. I'm looking for Jodi."

"That's me," she said brightly, giving me the once-over. "Welcome. Here's your new resident information. The key card inside will get you to your floor. At some point, I'll need to make a copy of your driver's license, but go ahead and get settled first."

"Thanks." I took the envelope from her hand, barely brushing her fingers with mine. Her face flushed pink.

"I'll be happy to take you up if you'd like."

"I think I can handle it." I smiled at her. Thought about asking for her number. Probably not a good idea to get involved with someone who had access to your apartment and could see you entering and leaving your building. Or to get involved with anyone at all, considering I came to New Orleans with a job to do.

"Nice to meet you, Jodi."

"Nice to meet you back." She giggled a little, and then bit her lip as she forced composure. "The elevator is to your right. The key card inside will—wait. I already said that."

"No worries," I said, flashing another smile. "Important information bears repeating."

"In that case, my name is Jodi. And I'm here Monday, Wednesday, and Friday afternoons."

"Duly noted."

I left the office, feeling her eyes on me as I went. I entered the elevator, pushed the button for the fourth floor, and put the flirting out of my mind. I stepped out of the elevator and opened the door to 4B.

The apartment wasn't empty.

"What the hell . . ."

"Come on in." Poe Sharpe sat on the couch. "Pardon me if I don't get up."

His bloodshot eyes were sunk deep in his pale face. His battered body held a liver that nearly took a nosedive and blood that had once belonged to someone else.

"What are you doing here? I thought you were still in ICU." I dropped my suitcases beside the door.

"Me being here is part of Paul and Liam's plan to keep me off Teague's radar. That's why they didn't tell you." The recently removed breathing tube left his voice scratchy, and fatigue made his accent heavy. "But, please, check with Liam to confirm. I would, if I were in your position."

I didn't want to be an asshole and jump for the phone, but I didn't want to get stabbed in my sleep, either.

"Really, I insist. I'll be right here. I've been a couch potato since I ported in. The recent skewering kind of took it out of me."

"Liam's getting ready to get on the plane for Nashville, so I'll go ahead and call." Flimsy excuse. I stepped out to the hall and dialed.

"You found Poe, I assume?" Liam asked, in lieu of saying hello.

"Maybe you could've warned me?" I paced back and forth. "Why is he in my apartment?"

"You're in his. When I visited Poe in the hospital at Vanderbilt, I asked a lot of questions, and he gave a lot of answers. The right answers."

I stopped, watching the arrows on the wall light up as the

elevators traveled from floor to floor. "I know he saved Em's and Michael's lives, but he's done some pretty damn questionable things, too, Liam."

"Here are the basics. Poe can give you details. When he helped Teague, he truly believed he was working for Chronos. She lied to him, and Jack manipulated his memories. When he discovered the truth and confronted them, Jack stabbed him. He ignored his injuries to save Em and Michael, and showed up on the front lawn of the Hourglass."

"Okay." An acknowledgment that I heard him, not that I understood.

"Your being in the apartment will help hide the fact he's there, as an excuse for lights and sounds and motion. He'll help you in any way he can, and you just have to believe me when I tell you that he's trustworthy."

"Okay," I repeated.

"I need a more coherent answer than that, Dune."

I heard the last call for the Nashville flight come over the airport loudspeaker and through the phone. "*Okay* is kind of all I've got at the moment."

"They're boarding my plane. Talk to Poe. Call me in a couple of hours if you want confirmation. All right?"

"All right."

Liam laughed. "At least it's not *okay*."

I stepped back into the apartment and looked at Poe. "So . . . hi."

"Hi."

"I'm sorry to crash, and thanks for the room. I wouldn't like recovering with someone new in my apartment."

"I wouldn't like moving into my new apartment and finding a roommate. You're providing a cover for me." Poe shrugged. "How about we're just mutually appreciative?"

I nodded and grabbed my bags.

Poe pointed to the left. "Your room is that way."

A light blue quilt covered the queen-sized bed. A walnut dresser stood against one wall, a matching desk on the other. I put my suitcases on the bed and wondered how much Chronos paid per job. How could one guy afford a two-bedroom in one of the nicest apartment buildings in the Garden District? Poe was nineteen, and he was living large. Really, really large.

I checked out the rest of the place. Hardwood floors linked a large living area with a kitchen. The walls were a soft yellow, and the furniture was low and modern, all in neutral colors. It smelled like laundry detergent and fabric softener. The spice rack was organized alphabetically. The canisters on the counter were arranged largest to smallest. A dishcloth and towel were both folded in exact thirds.

I went back into the living area. "You either have a maid, or you're OCD."

"Hope that's not a problem."

"So not a problem." I thrived on order. The pool house I'd been living in with Michael and Nate had been nice, but obviously overrun by teenage boys for a few years. This place made me feel like an adult.

"Thanks for keeping me off the streets." He readjusted his position on the couch pillows. "You interviewed with Paul today. And you start tomorrow?"

"Yes."

"I'm lucky he believed me and grateful to Liam for helping Paul understand that Teague and Jack tricked me. Paul Girard isn't the kind of guy you want on your bad side. Same goes for his daughter. And, by the way, Hallie doesn't know I'm back. We should probably keep it that way for a little while."

"You two were friends?"

"We still are, I hope. The hardest thing about all of this has been not being able to talk to her."

"Why can't you?"

"The less she knows, the safer she is. Teague has lied about everything. *Everything.* Your job is getting to the bottom of those lies, and I'll be happy to help you, if you want it."

I gazed down on the perfect, streetlamp-lit view of Saint Charles. The trolley whizzed by. My stomach jumped when I thought about meeting Hallie. "What's she like?"

"Demanding. Occasionally bitchy, but she has good reasons. Just so you're prepared, she has a way about her."

"What kind of way?" I asked.

"Sexy." Satisfaction ghosted across Poe's face. "Like you've never seen."

"You're together?"

"Friends. Hallie knows what she wants and how to ask for it. How to get it. I was fun, and that was it. She manages to play, even though she's basically trapped in that house. There was an accident a few years back. So now she goes on Chronos jobs, and she dances seriously. Otherwise, ivory tower."

"What about school?"

"Online. College classes. She finished high school at sixteen. She's a genius." Poe grinned. "All I can say is good luck."

A sneaky, sexy genius with a target on her back.

I'd need all the luck I could get.

Chapter 5

Hallie, One Week Later

"I told you, Dad. I don't need a bodyguard."

"As I've explained several thousand times, you are a minor. You live under my roof. You need what I say you need."

"He's creepy."

"How?"

"He looks at me."

"He's your bodyguard, Hallie. What's he supposed to look at? He's staying. I'm your father. What I say goes, and I'm done having this conversation."

I stepped out of Dad's office, slammed the door behind me, and turned my anger on the unreasonably hot yet still annoying bodyguard. "You"—I pointed a finger in his face—"are a complete pain in my ass."

He blinked and looked terrified, which was comforting, considering I was the one he was supposed to be protecting.

"Stay at least ten feet away. And stop looking at me."

I went through bodyguards the way insolent children went through nannies. It wasn't that I hated them personally; it was just that I didn't have anything else to do. It usually took me under a week to sneak out, lose their tail, and get them fired. This one chapped my ass more aggressively than most, because he was *inside* my house. Outside my room. Constantly around. Always watching. I expected today to be his last.

He followed me through the courtyard into the kitchen after my morning dance class, on my heels like a puppy at dinnertime, sealing his fate. I showered and went down to the kitchen in my robe. My shortest robe. Once I finished my yogurt, I scraped the bottom of the container for the last bite. He watched me walk to the trash can, step on the pedal, and dispose of the plastic.

"Oh." I tapped the silver spoon against my bottom lip. "Should I recycle?"

The only response was the controlled stare I'd learned to expect.

"Okay, then." I dropped my utensil in the sink and left the kitchen.

He was, of course, right behind me.

"Do you sleep?" I cast a glance over my shoulder. Pain in the ass or not, he was pretty to look at, with short black hair and a broad face. Gray green eyes with smile lines around them, though he couldn't have been over twenty. Maybe not shredded, but strong. His body had *presence*. "I only ask because you've been

67

here constantly. For three days. Don't you ever need to eat? How about pee?"

His lips twitched and I thought I'd won a smile, but he cut it off before it could bloom. I made sure to put a little swing in my step when I turned around to go upstairs.

He sighed and followed.

At the top, I spun around and caught him off guard. He grabbed at the curved banister to keep his balance. "Tell me something," I said. "Anything. I'll even settle for your name."

Stoic stance. No facial expression.

"Is my father paying you a crap ton of money not to talk or what?"

Now he focused on something behind me instead of me and leaned forward like he was ready to take another step.

I was all hands on hips, blocking his way. "Talk to me. About anything. The NFL? The NBA? Heck, the WWE?"

From the way his mouth shaped itself, I thought he could be biting the inside of his lower lip to keep from laughing.

"Have you been lobotomized?" I spoke slowly, with perfect enunciation, and mimicked sawing my own head open.

He gave his head a slight shake and stared at the floor. This time he couldn't stop the smile.

Gotcha.

"Look at that," I said. "Signs of intelligent life."

Maybe his brain muscle was as well developed as the rest of them.

"Are you going to your room," he asked, "or back down-stairs?"

"He has a voice!" A deep one. "Wherever you'll follow. That's where."

"I'm your bodyguard," he said in a monotone. "I have to follow you."

"To the ends of the earth."

"Your room or back downstairs?" he repeated.

In one quick movement, I reached up and pulled off his ear-piece. It slapped down against his chest. "Turn it off."

He clicked a button, and the green indicator light switched to red.

"I'm staying right here. You're going to talk to me," I said.

The downstairs door slammed shut. We both jumped, and his whole body tensed.

"Hallie?" Dad barked out the question.

"I'm here."

"Come down." Most everything Paul Girard said was a demand.

I didn't budge. "I just finished class, and I'm still in my robe."

"There's a guard with you?"

"Yeah. The new one who looks like a linebacker and stares at me while still managing to avoid direct eye contact."

He made it now. His grayish green peepers locked on to mine. The potential of disapproval from my father made him respond more quickly than any of my feminine posturing. I'd have to remember that.

Dad answered after a few seconds of silence. "I'll be waiting in the library."

"Library. Right."

Dad's fancy Italian loafers slapped across the hardwood floor. The sound echoed up the stairwell.

Once it disappeared, I stared at the male specimen in front of me. "Talk, or I'm not moving. I'm going to stand here until my dad comes looking for me. When he does, I'm going to untie my robe and back away from you like we've been doing something inappropriate. And just so you know, there's nothing under this silk but skin."

His Adam's apple convulsed in his throat.

"There's only one thing you can do to make me go in my room, put on my clothes, and get my fine ass to Daddy's office."

Silence.

"Tell me your name." I smiled. "That's all. Just your name."

The words came out so softly I couldn't hear him. I leaned in close and he made a strangled noise.

"Repeat that, please?"

"Junior. Ta'ala. But everyone calls me Dune."

"Where are you from, Dune?"

"I thought I only had to tell you my name."

I pulled at the tie of my robe, loosening the knot. It had been way too long since I'd had someone to amuse me, and I planned on taking full advantage.

"Samoa," he said in a rush.

I raised my eyebrows.

"Island in the South Pacific? Similar to Hawaii in landscape but less touristy?"

"I know where Samoa is," I said. "So you're Polynesian?"

"*Afatasi*. Half. My mom's from New Zealand."

"How did you end up here?"

"I needed a job, and I had to do something with . . . this." He looked very confused as he gestured to his big body.

My smile was slightly predatory. I had some ideas about what he could do with it.

"Are we done?" he asked, regaining composure. "You need to get to your father's library."

"We're done. For now."

I let the robe fall off my shoulders, making sure Dune saw a good bit of back before I closed the door to my room. Call me hard up for entertainment, but getting him fired was going to be fun.

Dad wanted me downstairs only to tell me he'd be out for the evening, which was the equivalent of a dangling carrot. I wanted to play with the bodyguard, but cabin fever was getting to me.

It was nice to have options.

I dressed in a bustier and a pair of red leather pants, pulled my hair back in a slick ponytail, and then climbed down the side of my house, courtesy of the decorative pattern of horizontal bricks. I didn't put on my stilettos until I was on the sidewalk, heading for the waiting cab. I plumped my lips on the ride over, gave the girls a little something extra, and changed my eye color to brown. I topped it off with a tiny, and definitely perky, button nose.

The cab dropped me at the corner of Bourbon and Saint Philip. I slipped into Lafitte's Blacksmith Shop.

Free. Breathing the air. Riding the rush.

I loved Lafitte's because it was dark; the tourists always put on a good show, and I appreciated the colorful pirate history. Built in the 1720s, it was the oldest bar in the country. Jean Lafitte had buried treasure under the open fireplace, and on occasion, he'd been known to show up in the flames to give a red-eyed glare to scurvy knaves interested in his loot. I ordered a cherry lime mojito and took a table in the corner by the bar.

Once my drink arrived, I pulled out the plastic sword loaded with fruit and popped a cherry into my mouth.

I almost choked on it when my bodyguard pulled away my glass. He had on a white long-sleeved shirt, a chocolate brown vest, and an ivy cap. Surprisingly delicious.

"You can't have that."

"The hell, you say." I tried to take the drink back, but he held it over my head. I couldn't reach it, even in my heels. "I thought I gave you the slip. I'm kind of impressed. What's your name again?"

"Dune." He sniffed my glass before fishing out a sliced lime and ripping the fruit away from the peel with his teeth. "Virgin."

"Says who?"

"I was talking about the drink." He slid my glass back onto my table.

"I wasn't."

He looked up, and I fingered the neckline of my bustier to see where his eyes would go. They stayed on my face.

Hmm. Passed the douche test.

"No one carded me," I said, "and I didn't offer to show ID, so of course it doesn't have alcohol. Bartenders are smart, especially in the Quarter."

"Here's an idea," he said. "How about you bottoms up with your citrus Shirley Temple and I'll take you back home?"

I sat back in my chair and took slow sips, studying him. He had a strong face, a wide jaw, and a bow-shaped upper lip. He smiled, because he realized I was staring at his mouth. I met his gaze.

His eyes were so damn *sweet*. There was no other word for it. His lashes were thick, and a scar sliced through his left eyebrow.

He was still smiling. Because I was still staring. I drained my drink. "I need another one."

"You sure you don't just want to grab a bottle of water at home?" he asked.

"Yessir."

"You're going to make this hard on me, aren't you?"

"Most definitely."

He reached for my glass and fished out the remaining cherry. "Here's an idea." He was smiling with his eyes again. "How about we negotiate?"

Dune

Chewing on the fruit gave me a second to gather my thoughts. I stared at her. "You look different."

An obvious statement, which was why it had to be said.

Hallie raised her brows and sucked on the end of the plastic sword that had been in her drink. Her hair was as dark as usual, but her normally hazel irises were a deep brown. "Do I now?"

The changes were subtle, because her body was slim and tall like usual, but something was off. "Yeah."

She smiled and leaned over to rest her elbows on the table. The angle and the bustier were doing a number on her cleavage. Her cleavage was doing a number on me—that was the difference. There wasn't usually so much of it. I made a great show of *not* looking.

"Not one bodyguard has been able to catch me once I got into the Quarter. I'm offended—maybe impressed—that you're here."

"You run away a lot?"

"Every chance I get."

"Why?"

"You've met my father."

Tossing the plastic sword onto the table, she stood up straight, giving up the attempt to draw me in, and finally allowing me the opportunity to breathe normally.

"He's not so bad." I shifted on my stool.

"Are you kidding me?" The once-over she gave me could've been an X-ray. "If you're in his corner, why haven't you already started dragging me home?"

Because you're lonely, and you aren't alone right now.

Relief I hadn't said it out loud made me a little light-headed. "I'm not a caveman. I don't drag. And I was hoping, maybe, I could convince you to go back with me by asking nicely."

"You aren't going to threaten to tell my dad? That's what they usually do: get all blustery and self-righteous and make a big point of how much trouble I'll be in when I get home." She shrugged. "But I never get in trouble, and they always do. You're smart, Dune Ta'ala from Samoa."

And just a few minutes ago, she'd acted like she couldn't remember my name. "I need this job."

She stepped closer and I caught the sparkles on her shoulders and neckline. "Are you trying to make me feel guilty?"

"No. Maybe." I needed her to move back. I needed to stay objective. I didn't need to know that she smelled like buttercream frosting. "Yes."

"So back to negotiations. Here's the deal. You stay here with me for a little while, let me have some fun, and we can go back together."

"I don't—"

"Take or leave it." She leaned forward again, so I stared at the ceiling.

I guessed I was taking it.

Hallie patted the seat beside her. I eyed it and remained standing, wondering if she sneaked some superglue onto the leather so she could make a quick escape.

"I really just want to take you home and get you to bed—"

"Keep walking into that innuendo. Really. I enjoy it."

"Get you to bed before your dad gets home so I don't get fired," I finished, with a sigh. "Please, Miss Girard?"

She put up a hand. "Hallie, if you want to stay on my good side."

"I'm deathly afraid of your bad side, Hallie."

Her next move stole my breath. She slid off her stool and put her palms on my chest, ran her hands down my stomach, and hooked one finger inside the waistband of my pants. "Do you dance?"

"I . . ."

A second finger sneaked in. She pulled me closer.

"Um . . ." I tried to step away.

"Just where do you think you're going?"

I thought of her bare back, skin as smooth as velvet, and how she must taste. I wondered how she'd respond if I gave in. How far things would go before I caught myself and remembered why I came to New Orleans.

Best to remember why I was here right now.

"Home. I'm taking you home."

"I could get you in a lot of trouble," she threatened, trying to play me. Even though I preferred girls who were a little more low-key, if I'd been a normal guy without some higher purpose, I'd have let her play me all the way out. "You're here. I'm here. Why can't we have fun?"

"You know why," I said.

"You aren't going to give in, are you?"

I shook my head. She picked up her bag and started for the other side of the bar. "Where do—"

"The bathroom. To change." She pointed to her red leather pants. "Did you want to help?"

I shook my head. "I don't want to help."

"Jean Lafitte likes to hang out in the ladies'." She flashed a wide smile. "Pirates. They never disappoint. Especially when I pretend they all look like Johnny Depp."

"Fine. Go change. *Don't* sneak out a bathroom window."

"I said I'd go home with you and I will."

I had no reason to trust her, but she didn't seem like a liar. A sneak, most definitely, but not a liar. "Forgive me if I have trouble taking you at your word."

"There aren't any windows in the bathroom." She growled in frustration. "You can check, unless you're afraid of pirates."

"It's not like you couldn't go in and come out a completely different person."

Her eyes narrowed and she sat back down. "What did you just say?"

"I mean, you have a proclivity for disguises. There's the shoes. And the eyelashes. The brown contacts. The outfit."

She shook her head. "Did my dad tell you anything about me?"

"All he said was that you had . . . an uncanny knack with appearances."

"An uncanny knack?"

In the span of a second, her face morphed back to its original form, her eyes to their original hazel. I was so fascinated by the transformation that I didn't react. Big mistake.

She spoke through her teeth. "Who the hell are you?"

"I . . ."

"I just transmutated."

When I didn't react, she huffed in frustration.

"Regenerated, shape-shifted, whatever. Point being, I changed my appearance, and you didn't freak." Now she leaned forward. "One more chance. Who. Are. You?"

The music stopped. There was one long beat of complete silence, and the dance music became a lively piano riff.

Behind Hallie, the aged wood of the walls lightened. Lafitte's used gas lamps instead of electric, but now the scent of grease candles filled the air. The smoke from the wicks grew thicker, heavy in the air.

The building's structure remained, but the furnishings became more rustic and newer at the same time. Subtle changes—lack of wear and tear on the floors and walls, the clothes people wore. The features of those living in the past blended with those in the present, and neither appeared to notice the other.

I felt as if I'd been on a merry-go-round for too long. I stood perfectly still while the world rushed by, and it left me unsettled.

"It doesn't know what to pick," Hallie murmured under her breath. "Past, present, never future. Eeny, meeny, miney, moe."

Men in loose white shirts with open collars sat along the bar, drinking and laughing. Seconds later, they were college girls with fruity drinks. Then they were both at the same time.

Hallie's attention jumped from the rips to me, mistrust immediately marring her features.

"You see them."

"See who?"

The accusation remained unsaid, but it hung there between us like frozen winter breath.

"Truth. Now." She leaned forward again, gripping the edge of the table. "Why are you here, and what do you know?"

Chapter 6

Hallie

He'd gone all college professor–like, with his fingers steepled together. "Bear with me for a second, and give me a chance to help you understand."

"Understand what?" The piano riff faded, replaced by a low, thrumming bass as things inside the bar returned to normal. "I can barely hear you over Jay-Z. Outside." I slid off my stool and grabbed my bag.

He took my elbow, and when the crowd got thicker as we approached the side door, he moved his hand to the small of my back. We stepped out into the cold. I shivered before he maneuvered me to stand beside one of the industrial-sized warming lamps.

Thoughtful. Considerate. Tricky.

The bass still thumped through the closed shutters of Lafitte's, but we were the only people in the courtyard. November wasn't the best time for outdoors, even as far south as New Orleans.

"All right," I said. "I'm ready. Shock and awe away."

"You aren't taking me seriously."

"That's kind of the way I roll, chief."

"Stop it. This is important."

His urgency startled me. I flinched when he put his hands on my shoulders. They were big and warm, and covered a lot of bare surface area.

"I'm sorry." He started to move his hands, but I grabbed his wrists.

"Uh-uh," I said. "It's too cold."

I liked the warmth and the feel of his skin against mine. He slipped his jacket off his shoulders and wrapped it around me.

That's when I noticed he wasn't packing heat.

That's when I got nervous.

"Why are you here?" I asked.

"I'm part of your security detail."

"Security details carry weapons."

He hedged. "I wasn't sure of the carrying laws in Louisiana. Not in a bar."

"Laws don't matter when you work for Paul Girard. You do what he says."

"I'm new at the security thing, and if you don't let me take you home, I'll never get a chance to be old at it." His eyes told me he was worried about way more than losing his job.

"I'll let you take me home." His look of relief disappeared when I held up my hand. "When you tell me who you are."

I watched him mentally backpedal, then scramble around for a good answer. It didn't take too long.

"You were right." He exhaled deeply, his shoulders slumping. "Your dad told me about your transmutation ability."

"Smooth. Totally nonobvious subject change." Maybe I'd been wrong about the smart thing. "Don't even try to play like that's all you know."

"You aren't the only person in the world with time-related abilities."

He shouldn't have seen what we saw inside Lafitte's. And he shouldn't know about people with time abilities.

"Do you have your own brand of magical powers?" I fisted my hands on my hips. "Is that why he told you about me?"

"Yes. No." He ran his hands over his short hair, and then repeated it, like he forgot what it felt like.

"Do you work for Chronos?"

"No, not Chronos."

He could see ripples. He knew about time-related abilities. Nothing shocked him, even my quick change from one face to another. Then I remembered something Dad said.

"You work for the Hourglass." I whipped his jacket off my shoulders and shoved it into his chest.

His face and his fumble gave him away. "Wh—what?"

"Please *do not* irritate me further by acting like you don't

82

know what I'm talking about. That would be a serious mistake."

"I used to work for the Hourglass, but now I work for your dad."

"And they sent you?" I asked. "Were there no competent adults available?"

He stared at me for a long time. "I know more about certain subjects than others. Even competent adults."

A sneaking suspicion crept its way up my spine. "What kind of subjects?"

"Subjects like you."

"Right." I started backing up toward the gate that led out to Bourbon.

"Hallie, wait, please."

I stopped when I saw his eyes. They couldn't keep a secret. Honesty shone out from behind them.

"You're more than you think you are, and your ability is only a symptom of something . . . greater." He took a steadying breath. "Something huge. Something that could possibly change the world, even save it. I can help you."

I laughed. So hard I doubled over.

"I don't think you're grasping the magnitude of what I'm trying to tell you," he said seriously.

"What I will be grasping are your man berries in a vise when I turn you over to my dad."

"He knows who I am and where I'm from. He hired me to help you."

"Dad knows who you are?" That straightened me right up. "And he made you my bodyguard? Because you're really, really crappy at it."

"I tracked you here, didn't I?"

Touché.

"It was his cover for me. And you weren't supposed to be leaving the house, so I wasn't supposed to need to be good at it. But I put a GPS in your bag."

I smacked him with my purse and then held it open. "Get it out. Now."

After he removed the GPS and slipped it into his pocket, he looked at Lafitte's, back at me, and then blew out a deep breath. "I'm really kind of like . . . a historian."

"I'm an Aquarius."

He groaned in frustration.

"So you're here to make a historical note of what?" I shivered, rubbed my arms, and jerked the jacket back out of his hands, shoving my arms into the sleeves.

"I'm not here as a witness. My specialty is in something called the Infinityglass. I used to think it was a what. Now I know it's a who. And you're it."

He looked at me as if he expected a big gasp, or some sort of physical reaction. I didn't give him one.

"Hold up a second, Hagrid." Laughter bubbled to the surface again. "If you think you're here to tell me how special I am, you can stop. I already know."

84

"You what? But . . . how?"

"Did you really think you were springing something on me?" I hugged myself, wrapping his jacket around my body. "That's cute. Were you going to teach me the ways of the world, Obi-Wan? Did you think you were my only hope?"

I expected him to crumble under the weight of my sarcasm. Instead, he rested his shoulder against the outer wall of Lafitte's, and looked all sorts of superior. And knowledgeable. "What if I am?"

His confidence carried knowledge instead of swagger. All I had was enough information to be dangerous.

"How much do you know about who you are, Hallie? Because I bet I know more."

I shrugged and tried not to look like my next breath depended on hearing what he knew.

"Give me twenty-four hours," he said. "I promise I can help you."

"I can't . . . I have to think about this." I turned to head for the gate to the sidewalk.

And faced a ripple.

The man in front of me had lanky brown hair. His clothes were old-fashioned, but dusty, not dirty. Authentic. Real or part of a vision, his eyes were black and devoid of emotion.

"Things are hopping tonight." I slid my arms out of Dune's jacket.

Dune grabbed at me. "Wait, Hallie."

"Just go around it." I jerked away from Dune, still gripping the jacket, and took one fat step forward. So did the rip.

We became one. The present was lost. The Bourbon Street I knew slipped away. Cars were replaced with horse-drawn buggies, and daylight replaced dark. My body didn't belong to me. Neither did my mind.

A memory I had no right to tickled the edge of my conscious.

"I've done no wrong. I didn't mean to. It was an accident."

My voice, but not my voice.

"It was a mistake."

Suddenly, a man stands across from me, rage touching every one of his features. "You killed her."

Callused hands scrape the thin skin of my neck.

My skin, but not my skin.

My coat smells of wood smoke, and the breath of the man choking me reeks, moist against my face. I squeeze the man's wrists so hard I hear bones pop. I am surprised by my strength.

"You're an abomination," the attacker accuses.

A kitchen maid. A new one, with a gap between her front teeth. What I'd done wasn't an accident. The swamp had stunk of rotting fish and algae in the late summer air. I hadn't even pushed her skirt down before I rolled her into the water.

"I didn't mean to," I say inside my head, silently begging, as black dots cloud my vision.

I pushed against the memory, wanting out of the man's mind. I focused on escape with all I had. We separated with force, and he stumbled into a veil that hung in the air, shining like sunlight on water. It was jagged around the edges, and the inside was nothing but swirling darkness.

The dark disappeared, zipping from top to bottom. It left no suggestion of the incident, with the exception of a faint hint of wood smoke.

I managed to stay upright for five seconds before the ground made a grab for my face.

Dune

The rip . . . absorbed Hallie.

It couldn't have lasted for more than fifteen seconds, but it felt like an hour. I knew I was looking at Hallie, because her clothes didn't change. At first, I wondered if it were a transmutation thing, if maybe she were trying to mess with me to make me leave her alone.

But her features rearranged themselves.

A broad forehead and small eyes took over Hallie's face, unseeing. Thin lips formed words, something about a mistake. At first, anger distorted the expression, but it quickly turned to horror, and then the skin began to turn blue.

I was reaching out for her when Hallie's facial features became more prominent, and she and the rip separated. She spun around, and almost as if she shoved him, the man fell backward into the veil, shimmering in the air. It zipped shut behind him.

I caught Hallie just before she hit the ground. We were still in the courtyard of Lafitte's. After a quick check of the windows to search for peering eyes, I scooped her up in my arms and scanned the area for someplace safe. Going back into Lafitte's wasn't an option.

"Cab," she said groggily, pushing herself out of my arms. "Get a cab and take me home."

I flagged down a cab and helped her in, giving the driver the address to her house. I put my arm around her shoulders and pulled her to my chest. Let the driver think we were making out. He'd seen her. I'm sure he wouldn't blame me.

"Are you okay?" I whispered into the hair above her ear. "Is there anything I can do?"

She hung on to the front of my shirt and tilted her chin to look up. "No. But thanks for catching me."

"What did you see?"

"You first. What did you see?"

Her jaw had gone slack, her eyes blank, and her limbs loose. "You were limp, staring out at the dark like you could see something playing out in it."

Hallie nodded and then shivered. "I could."

"Your face . . . it was like you lost yourself for a minute." I didn't want to tell her how much her features had changed. "Then you and the guy separated."

"I did." A deep wrinkle formed between her brows.

"Then the veil went dark." Or sewed itself shut. I didn't want to say it, because it sounded too crazy, and we were running high on crazy already.

She nestled into me and held on tighter. "I became someone else. A man, one who'd done terrible things, and another man was choking me. Then I was me again, and I . . . pushed."

"Has anything like that ever happened to you before?"

"No." I heard fear in her voice. I'd known her for a week, and I was certain Hallie Girard didn't do fear. "You're the expert. Can you explain it?" she asked.

"I don't know the answer." A primal drive kicked in when I looked into her eyes. "But I will."

"I believe you."

We reached her house. I paid the driver and helped her out of her seat. She held on to my arm, just until the cab drove off, and then she pulled away, promptly hitting the sidewalk on her knees.

"Damn!" She went on her palms next, uttering several more curse words.

Hallie prized her independence and I wanted to give it to her, but she was in obvious pain. I dropped to a squat beside her, resting my elbows on my knees, my hands outstretched.

"I'm not leaving you. I can help you get to your house, or at the very least, I can walk behind you. Whatever you want."

"I don't want anything." She bit her lower lip as she stared at my hands. "From anyone. I can handle situations by myself. Usually. This . . . this is . . . different."

I reached out farther. "It's five minutes of assistance, just enough to get you to your room."

"My room, huh? Are you trying to get another flash?"

"Not tonight. I won't make any promises about tomorrow." I smiled, and watched as the teasing softened her. When she smiled back, my heart gave an extra kick in my chest.

Hallie took my hands and I helped her stand. She held on tight, and when we reached her house, she stopped at the side entrance.

"I'll take it from here," she said. "Carl's on duty, and he won't rat me out or ask any questions. Thanks for getting me home."

"So, tomorrow. Do you want me to come back, or are you planning to . . . what was it? Put my man berries in a vise and hand me over to your dad?"

Her laugh was soft, her eyes curious. We looked at each other, and in that long moment, we came to an understanding.

"Yes," she said. "Come back tomorrow."

Chapter 7
Hallie

*D*ad's bedroom door was open.

"You did it," I said from the hall, "again."

Even though it was almost midnight, he still had on his tie. His holster and gun sat on the top of his dresser. I knew the safety was on. For the millionth time, I started to wonder what drove him to constantly arm himself inside his own home, but stopped.

The answer was my mother.

He gestured me inside. "I did what again?"

I'd showered and changed. My knees were completely healed, but my legs still felt wobbly. From my fall. Not from nerves.

I sat down in the armchair by the window. Bulletproof glass, of course. "You brought somebody in to handle business you should've taken care of yourself."

He didn't look at me, just loosened his tie.

"Dune knows I'm the Infinityglass. So do you."

Now Dad spun around to face me head-on. "He told you that?"

"No, Daddy," I said softly. "Mom did."

Sadness came into him slowly, pulling down his shoulders and the corners of his mouth. I hated to watch him carry regret for her choices. She'd thrown us off so carelessly, and he'd tried to make up for her absence. He'd really tried.

I wanted to spare him any more pain, but I wanted the truth, too. "Why didn't you tell me?"

Dad turned his back, took off his belt, and untucked his shirt. "I don't know enough. Definitely not the kind of answers you're going to want. When did your mother tell you?"

"She called and offered to help, all motherly-like. It was the same day you told me about Poe being in the hospital. About his betrayal with her."

He grimaced. "We must have been on her mind."

"There's a first time for everything." I focused on some loose threads at the bottom of my Lady Gaga T-shirt.

"Poe . . . I might have been too harsh. I don't know if he knew what he was doing when he helped your mother."

"He's been in the hospital, but he hasn't even called. That's a pretty good sign he's hiding something."

Dad just frowned.

"How did you find out about the Infinityglass and . . . me?"

He picked up his ever-present glass of Maker's Mark. "Gerald Turner. He'd been doing some research, and he found some things."

Gerald Turner had been my godfather, and a professor at Bennett University in Memphis. He'd also been murdered in October. "What kinds of things?"

"Clues that the Infinityglass was human, and that the specific gene for it is dormant." Dad frowned and fiddled with the top button of his dress shirt. He wasn't a fiddler. "For the Infinity-glass gene to become—activated, for lack of a better word—he or she had to come into contact with something that triggered a genetic response, a stressor that kicked that specific gene into overdrive."

"Dr. Turner just called you, out of the blue, to talk about the Infinityglass? And Mom called me to talk about it, too. He lived in Memphis; Mom's been operating out of Memphis. That's not a coincidence at all."

"Neither was the timing of his death."

The implications weighed heavily on me, and from the lines on Dad's face, he felt them, too.

"Gerald and I talked about Liam Ballard and the Hourglass. He believed they were trustworthy. Then Liam confirmed Gerald's claims that you were the Infinityglass. I guess your mother telling you reinforces it again."

"And then you hired the Hourglass, and they sent you Dune."

"He's gone." When Dad set his jaw, I knew I was in for a fight. "He wasn't supposed to tell you anything. He broke our agreement."

"Dad, you can't. Things happened to us that blew his cover. It's not like he just started spewing information."

"Intentional or not, he still broke our agreement."

"Our only other option for answers is Mom," I argued. "Dune has information that you want and I need. He said he was working for you instead of Hourglass now."

"He was supposed to be, but I'm not sure he's competent."

I thought about the way Dune had reacted so calmly to the rip, my sudden face change, and the possession. A lesser man would have pissed himself and then run like hell. Not only had he stuck, he'd helped me get home without making me feel needy.

And he really did have the sweetest eyes I'd ever seen. He smiled with his eyes as much as he blinked. He was solid. It was a gut feeling, and I always went with my gut feelings.

"He is." I surprised myself with my own vehemence. "If you don't believe it, give him a job to do, let him prove himself. He pulls it off; your faith is restored. Even better, give him a job that stretches him a little. One that requires him to put his Goody Two-shoes morality aside."

"You're talking about the Bourbon Orleans job."

"Since Poe's out of the picture, you don't have anyone else to do it, and if I recall, the finder's fee was hefty. It would be a shame to cancel it now." I leaned over and gave him big, innocent eyes. "He won't have to do much, and I'll be perfectly safe. You *did* hire him to be a bodyguard."

"He wasn't supposed to ever leave the house with you."

"He found me in the Quarter and brought me home, didn't he?" I felt a twinge of guilt that I hadn't given Dad the whole story about what happened outside Lafitte's, but deciding what information to share and what to withhold from him was a constant struggle. It sucked to need leverage with your own father, but it was what it was.

"You drive a hard bargain, kid." He shook his head. "You did learn from the best."

"So you aren't going to fire him?"

My father considered me for a long moment. "Why does this matter so much to you?"

"We've been walking around for days keeping a secret from each other that basically everyone knows. I'm the Infinityglass. Besides my waste-of-space mother, he's my best chance for finding out exactly what that means. That's why you hired him in the first place, right? Because he's supposed to know the most?"

Dad nodded.

"There you go. Plus, I think that if his balls are big enough for him to show up at work tomorrow after he blew his cover tonight, he might be more of an asset than either one of us expects. Am I right?"

"I'd prefer not to hear you talk about his . . . balls." Dad winced as he said it. "But you're right. If he comes back, I'll send him with you on the hotel job."

"Thanks, Dad. And no more balls. Swear."

"Go," he said, pointing at the door.

But he was smiling.

Dune

Exercise had become a thing.

Since I'd discovered the Infinityglass was human, I'd read and reread every piece of information I could understand. I'd sorted it all into neat lists, spreadsheets, and folders on my desktop. I'd stared at it for so long I didn't know what it said anymore.

Until I walked away.

The pounding of my feet on the pavement, the clanking of free weights landing in the rack, the swooshing sound of the elliptical—all of them made my mental calculations and deductions clearer. Connections flowed as freely as sweat, and the million-piece puzzle I had to solve became manageable.

❦

My phone rang as I was leaving the apartment to go down to the gym.

"Dune! What's up?" It was Michael, returning my call. I didn't waste time on pleasantries.

"There's some weird stuff happening here, and I wanted to see if you were experiencing it in Ivy Springs, too." I opted for the stairs instead of the elevator. "Have you guys noticed changes with the rips since I left?"

"They're more complex. Bigger." He was quiet for a few seconds. "I feel like the tear in time used to bleed like a paper cut, and now we're at full hemorrhage. What about there?"

"Same. But . . ." I paused, tried to figure out how to phrase my next question. "Have any of the rips tried to take over?"

"Take over how?" He sounded as grave as I felt.

"People. Possession."

He proceeded to say more curse words in fifteen seconds than I'd heard him say in the past five years. "What the hell happened?"

"It was Hallie. I've never seen anything like it or read anything about it. Her face, her voice took on different characteristics. The rip . . . moved in." I stopped walking and lowered my voice. "She relived a murder."

"You need to tell Liam."

"Not yet. Give me a couple of days. It could've been a fluke thing or an Infinityglass-specific thing, and I want to know for sure." I started back down the stairs. "Let's see if it happens to anyone else first."

"I defer to your wisdom," Michael said. "But you know I'm a phone call away."

"Ditto, brother."

I hung up and pushed open the door to the gym to find Poe climbing off the treadmill. There was a towel hanging over the security camera.

"How's the rehab going?" I asked.

"Slow." He pulled another towel off the stand beside the water dispenser and wiped his face. "Want to spot me?"

I laughed. "You want to pop your stitches?"

"I'll spot you instead." Poe pointed to the weight stack as I got into position on the bench. "Four hundred?"

"Three." Silently, I hoped that much wouldn't kill me.

He loaded three forty-five pound weights on each side. Three-fifteen, including the bar. I was going to end up with a hernia.

"When I choke to death on this bar and you have to spot me, how is that going to help your liver heal?" I asked.

"It won't. So don't drop the weight."

The first five were easy. The next four were brutal. Poe almost had to spot me on ten, and by the time I lowered the bar, my arms felt like stretched-out gummy bears.

"I need to talk to you about Hallie," I said, sitting up.

"Upstairs. I need a fix." He grabbed the towel covering the camera as he teleported out, and I took the normal route to the apartment, using the elevator this time. I found him in the kitchen digging a giant box of Popsicles out of the freezer. "You want?"

"I'm good," I said, leaning back against the counter as he took out four and put the rest away. "Hungry?"

"I'm trying to come off the pain meds. I feed my sugar addiction instead. What's up?"

Now that I'd broached the subject, I hesitated. I knew there had been something between Hallie and him once, but I also sensed that the friendship that replaced it was stronger.

"It was a simple question." Poe pulled a Popsicle from a wrapper. Grape. He bit off the end. "Don't blow a brain gasket."

"I'm just standing here trying to figure out if I can trust you."

"I know where you sleep. If I wanted to cause you harm, it would already be a reality, yeah?"

"Glad you've thought about it."

Poe smiled.

"Okay," I conceded. "Something happened last night. I blew my cover. She figured out I work for the Hourglass, or that I used to, anyway."

"She's too smart for her own good." He slid the wrapper off another Popsicle. "Then what?"

I told him how the ripple had absorbed Hallie and taken her over, the way the veil seemed to zip closed behind her.

"Damn it." Poe slammed his fist down onto the counter. "I should never have agreed not to call her, but I wanted to keep her out of it. Was she okay?"

"Yeah, she was. Shaken, but okay."

"I need to help." The pleading in his eyes was honest.

"I don't know. . . ."

"Please. I have to do something. I've watched every episode of *Doctor Who*. Ever. Exhausted every series of everything I can find online. My next stop is reality TV, and, Dune, I just can't go there. We're talking about Hallie. She's my best friend."

"I've spent so much time with the Skroll that I don't know

what's up or down anymore." I put one arm behind my head and stretched out my biceps, then moved to my triceps, watching him. And then I relented. "Ever since that night, I've thought about giving you a crack at it."

"Are you serious?"

"As serious as a heart attack."

"I've only read the Skroll once. I'd be happy to get another shot at it, especially the newly translated stuff."

"I thought you couldn't get it open," I said.

"Sure I could. I just didn't tell Teague. At least I was coherent enough to know not to trust her with that."

"Most of the information I have is inherited from my dad. Stuff he gathered for years."

"It's different from what's on the Skroll?"

"Parts of it, yes."

"Well," Poe drawled, "are you going to tell me what you want me to look for, or are you going to make me guess?"

"How about we start with an explanation for the possession?"

"I can do that." He ate the last bit of Popsicle and returned the others to the freezer. "I guess that means you're trusting me, then?"

"Two sets of eyes are better than one," I said. Truthfully, four. I was going to put Liam and Michael on it, too. I'd uploaded the Skroll to a highly protected server. The same kind the CIA used.

"Lay it on me," Poe said, throwing the wooden stick in the trash. "Everything."

Chapter 8
Dune

When I got ready to leave for work that afternoon, Poe had his computer and a ton of index cards out, already searching through the information I'd given him.

He wore a huge pair of wayfarer glasses, and was so Anthony Head, circa *Buffy the Vampire Slayer*, that it was all I could do not to call him Giles.

"Anything you want me to look for besides the possession connection?"

"*Possession connection.* That sounds like a really screwed-up PBS kids' show." I grabbed my own computer. "Just that I'm still looking for the thing that kicked Hallie into overdrive. Whatever the genetic stressor was. Maybe keep an eye out for that, too."

He nodded and dropped his eyes to focus on his computer. "Will do."

I took the trolley down Saint Charles, even though the walk would've helped clear my head. Hallie had said she wanted me to come back today, but if she'd changed her mind, told her father that I'd blown my cover . . . I'd be screwed. Possibly dead. I had a brief vision of Paul Girard and his gun holster.

I jumped off at my trolley stop and approached the side entrance to the Girard house slowly. No attempts were made on my life, so I checked in with Carl, the head of security, made my way to Hallie's room, and knocked on her door. It flew open.

"You. You're here."

"I'm here." I scanned the hallway to the right and left of her bedroom door. "Were you expecting someone else?"

"No. I just . . ."

"You thought I wouldn't come back."

"It crossed my mind. I wondered if what happened last night freaked you out enough to make you cut and run. If the nice-guy stuff was for real."

"It is, just like my fear that your dad would be waiting for me at the front door." I grinned. "Did you reach a verdict on my nice-guy status?"

"Still out." She tilted her head and paused. "Hung jury."

I nodded. "If the jury reaches a decision, I'll be out here. Doing something bodyguardlike."

The left corner of her mouth tipped up a fraction of an inch. "But you aren't a fake bodyguard anymore."

"I am to your dad."

She grinned.

"You *told* him? And I'm still breathing?"

"I can be very persuasive."

I had no doubt about that. "Okay. I guess I'll just . . . stand here until you make a decision."

"I was thinking." She opened her door wider. "Maybe we need to spend some quality time together."

I started backing up. "I'm not coming in your room. No need to give your dad more reasons to come after me with a shotgun, even if we are just talking about science."

"He leans more toward the smaller firearms. Besides, I have an idea."

"Which is?" I asked cautiously.

"If we're going to get to know each other—well, what each of us knows about this situation, anyway—how about we play a game of either-or?"

It seemed innocent, but I knew Hallie had a penchant for being tricky, and I liked being alive. "What are the terms of this particular game? Are we talking personal or professional questions?"

"Both." She gave me the once-over. "I'd like to know who I'm getting in bed with. So to speak."

God, the girl was wicked. I was probably in trouble. "Fine. Books or movies?"

She raised one eyebrow, surprised that I was willing to dive right in. "Movies."

"Downloads or CDs?"

"Records," she answered in a drawn-out voice, like I was an imbecile.

I continued. "Vanilla or chocolate?"

"Strawberry." She turned it around. "What about you?"

"Butter pecan."

"Boxers or briefs?" This came with a grin.

"Neither."

I watched as her eyes wandered in the direction of my waistband. When she knew she'd been busted, her cheeks got a little pink.

Clearing her throat, she asked, "Beach or mountains?"

I blanched. She caught it.

"You have an immediate comeback for your underwear choice, but beach or mountains stumps you." She tapped her lips with one finger and studied me. "Why is it a hard question?"

"Mountains."

"No." She leaned against her door frame. "I asked you why that's hard to answer."

"I don't think you know how to play either-or. There aren't supposed to be explanations, just one-word answers."

"My house," she said. "My rules. Tell me why you're avoiding."

I straightened my shoulders. "It has to do with my special brand of magical powers."

"Which are?" When I didn't respond, she said, "You don't have to tell me, Dune. But I'd like to know."

I sensed we'd reached the tipping point of our tentative alliance.

I answered because she gave me the opportunity not to, and because her authenticity peeked out from behind her curiosity. "Tides. I can control the tides. Water in its many forms. We think that I can affect moon phases as well, but it's not the kind of thing you can test."

"That's . . . wow. That's pretty serious."

"It's okay on a small scale, because I understand how to control it, even though I rarely let other people see me do it. Tiny things like plumbing leaks or condensation, not a problem at all. Ponds, contained bodies of water that I can see end to end— wide open and easy to handle, as long as they're people free. Streams, creeks—those are doable, but aren't ideal. Lakes and rivers. Possible, but also possibly catastrophic. I avoid them altogether. And oceans . . . well. I haven't been to the ocean since I was eleven."

"Why? Same offer stands. You don't have to tell me."

Growing up in American Samoa had its advantages. For me, it was the Pacific Ocean. I used to race over the dunes to get to the water when I was a kid—hence my nickname. The moon's gravitational force drew the tide, and the tide drew me, pulling me to the ocean over and over again.

When I was eleven, I pulled back.

"I was at the beach, on a picnic with my family. Understand, in Samoa, everyone is family. That's just the way villages work.

Warm sun, cool breeze, good food. We laughed a lot. Anytime we were all together, there was music."

Such a simple thing, my hands in the water. The rush that ran through my extremities, the way my pulse tuned itself to the crashing of the waves. The water became an extension of my fingers; when I waved them to the left, the fish swam that direction. When I moved them to the right, they followed.

"I'd been able to manipulate the current ever since I was little. I always wanted to see fish up close. Not the tiny minnows that were always by the shoreline, but the big kind fishermen would bring back from excursions and hold up to have their pictures taken." I knew most of those were eventually stuffed, and probably left to gather dust while hanging on a wall somewhere in Middle America. "I didn't want to turn the fish into trophies. I just wanted to see them."

Hallie crossed her arms over her chest. "Any kid with an ability like that would."

"So, that day, I concentrated a little harder than usual, curling my fingers in toward my body.

"The waves came at me in a rush, so big, filling my mouth, eyes, nose, throat. I remember the way the salt burned. I couldn't breathe. Everything went black. When I woke up, my mom was on her knees in the sand, holding me. A trail of dead marine life stretched as far as I could see. Fish, with their scales drying up. Bloated jellyfish. A couple of dolphins, a shark. Giants, just . . . abandoned on the sand."

Hallie covered her mouth with her hands.

"There were also people. Lifeless bodies, covered with beach towels. I'd created a tidal wave. Even the strongest swimmers hadn't been able to fight it. Eleven members of my extended family died that day, one to represent each year of my life." I took a deep breath. Then another. "One of them was my father."

She stepped out of her room and took my arm. "Sit."

We sat down with our backs against the wall, shoulders almost touching.

"I haven't told anyone that story since I first came to the Hourglass." Liam first, and eventually, Nate. That had been over five years ago. I hadn't given either one of them details, and I wasn't sure why I had given them to Hallie now. "I know it was an accident, but sometimes the guilt can sneak up on me. My dad was a great guy. It was a rough loss for everyone."

"Tell me about him." She slid her legs out and crossed them at the ankles.

"He worked at Mauna Kea, at one of the big observatories. He was gone a lot. Fascinated by space and its relation to time. He knew about my ability, but never talked to me about it."

Instead, he wound the truth into fairy tales, as parents do when they believe reality is too frightening or too hard to comprehend. When we'd buried him, I knew the fairy tales he'd spent his life chasing were true. And over.

"My mom brought me mainland, and then I met Liam. Samoans have a word, *fa'a Samoa*. It means the 'Samoan way.'

Families extend beyond blood. I have that with the Hourglass."

Hallie took my hand in hers, and held it without saying a word. The line between business and friendship blurred. The neck of my T-shirt felt too tight.

"So that's why I'd choose the mountains." I cleared my throat. "Because I don't think I can ever go back to the ocean."

Hallie

Controlling tides. Moon phases. The loss of so many people who were important to him. He'd bared his soul, and the way his big shoulders curled over his chest made my heart hurt. I had to take his hand.

And I had to tell him my secret.

"It's nothing like losing a parent, but my best friend died a few years ago." The words came out before I could think about them, but they felt right instead of impulsive. "I don't usually talk about that, either."

He waited, holding my hand, and keeping those sweet eyes focused on my face.

"His dad was a bodyguard for us. I was still in public school at that point, but Dad had started to rein in nonschool activities. He had a new sense of paranoia that started spilling over into my life. His name was Benny. We'd been arguing, about something stupid like jelly bean flavors, or manga versus anime."

"That's what friends do," Dune said.

Fifteen and sneaky, thinking we could hide in the crowd lining Jackson Square, pretending my father's reputation didn't walk in front of me, or that his square jaw didn't hang all ridiculous on my baby-fat face. Pretending I wasn't a shiny red target with a wide-open bull's-eye.

The spires of Saint Louis Cathedral had stretched up toward the clouds like those on Cinderella's castle. No magic below, though, just busy crowds. Tourists held chicory coffee from Café du Monde in to-go cups; heat met crisp winter air and formed steam. At least there'd been no heat to exacerbate the leftover smells from a Saturday night in the Quarter. I'd tugged at the ends of my much-regretted pixie cut that were sticking out from underneath my skull cap. It had only made my ruler-straight body look more androgynous. Delayed puberty, my nemesis.

"Benny and I met when he came to work with his dad one day. I told him his belly looked like Santa's, he told me my lips were too big for my head, and I kicked him. We wrestled each other to the ground before the fight was broken up, but my father had seen me laugh. And Benny got to come back. Immediate besties."

Except for right before the accident, when he'd started doing things like offering up his jacket, letting me go first, opening doors. I thought maybe he was trying to make the move from five years of comfortable friendship into something unknown and scary.

"The shots were so loud. I thought they were fireworks at

first. I didn't understand why anyone would be setting fireworks off in the middle of the day. But it was gunfire."

Bullets had peppered the wrought iron and the sidewalk, scattered the crowd like jacks. Screams would serve as background noise for every waking moment of my next two years. Benny's blood would be the backdrop. His blue eyes were open and empty as I lay beside his wasted body, splattered by his blood. It was in that second, before reality and grief rolled in, I decided I'd spend the rest of my life living enough for both of us.

I met Dune's eyes. "He died right there on Jackson Square."

"Were you hurt?"

"Took a hit on my shoulder. I didn't know a bodyguard was tailing us, but he tackled me to get me to the ground, and broke my left leg in three places."

"I'm so sorry."

"Fifteen." I shrugged. "That's when I decided life was short—at least I'm pretty sure mine will be—and that there's no point in living if you don't go balls to the wall with it. Hard to do when you're protected the way I am, but it doesn't mean I'll stop. I turn eighteen soon."

"Will you leave home?" He understood. I could hear it.

"I want to go to school at Tulane, for dance. I understand why Dad wants me here, protected all the time. It was hard on everyone when we lost Benny. If he could just give me a little more lead on my leash . . . but he won't." I met his eyes. "I haven't decided what to do yet. If one day I'll change my appearance and run, or if I'll stay. But honestly, I can't see the latter as an option."

"I don't think anyone would blame you."

"No running today." I faced him, trying to lighten things up. If I kept talking, I'd turn my hallway into a confessional and Dune into my priest. "We still have a game to play."

"Agreed. But I'll only answer if you promise to keep undergarment preferences out of it."

He knew exactly how raw I felt, and how telling him so much so fast had surprised me. Instead of taking advantage of it, he helped me steer my emotions back to safe waters.

"Bikinis," I said, smiling. "Just so you know."

Chapter 9

Dune, Early December

*H*allie said, "So yes or no?"

It had been just over a week since I'd blown my cover, and Hallie and I had spent it playing an extended game of either/or in the hall outside her room. We'd talked about everything.

Except the Infinityglass.

Today we'd hit on all the major religions before she asked me to eat a late breakfast with her.

"How could I refuse? No, I mean, I really can't. Not you. You're the boss."

She popped up off the ground and held out her hands like she was going to help me up.

"Are you serious? I outweigh you by at least a hundred pounds."

She rolled her eyes and held out her hands in a more exaggerated way instead of answering, so I gave in. She pulled me up so easily we had an accidental chest bump. The grin she gave me when we made contact was full of suggestion.

Talk about conflict.

The Infinityglass started as a thing, then a person, and then morphed into a vibrant personality, but the past two weeks had humanized Hallie in a way I hadn't been prepared for. I still didn't know enough about her, but now it was on a hundred different levels, and they didn't even include the scientific angle. This was probably not good.

"How do you feel about bacon?" She pulled a strand of dark hair around her finger, twisting and untwisting.

"Passionate." I followed her down the stairs.

"I knew you had good taste. Speaking of passions, you never told me how you got interested in the Infinityglass in the first place."

I followed her into the kitchen.

"My dad. In the bedtime stories he told me, the Infinityglass was shaped like an hourglass, and the sands inside were powerful. They could reverse time, stop it, speed it up. It could transfer abilities between people who had a time-related gift. It had unknown magic that could be used to cure all the world's ills."

She turned away from me and opened the bread box. "The perfect fantasy story."

"I know how goofy that sounds, especially now that I've met you. Unless you're full of sand."

"I'm full of something, but it ain't sand."

She was joking, but the set of her shoulders told me that something I'd said bothered her. "The stories are a good memory of my dad. I always imagined going on an adventure with him to find the Infinityglass, kind of the way people chased the Holy Grail."

She popped four pieces of bread in the toaster and said, "I fart in your general direction."

"What?"

"*Monty Python. Holy Grail.* 'I fart in your general direction.' You need an education, big boy."

"I know *Monty Python and the Holy Grail.*" The girl continued to impress while simultaneously throwing me off my game. "I just can't believe *you* know it."

"I never leave my house, remember? Movies—good movies—are my friends." She took jelly out of the fridge and honey from the cupboard, put the jars on the table, and leaned against the edge. "I have to apologize. We're out of bacon."

"You don't have to make me breakfast," I said.

"Sure I do. My humanity stole your quest potential. I feel like I owe you."

"The quest just looks different than I thought it would." A lot different. "It's more complicated than I expected it to be."

"It sure is." She stared at me for a long time.

I stared back.

The toast popped up and we both jumped.

"I'm sorry I've put it off for so long. So you'll understand my head space: loyalty is an issue." Hallie buttered the toast before offering me two pieces.

I took the bread. "I don't blame you, and I'd feel the same in your situation. But if we approach this logically, you have to tell me what you *do* know, or I can't help you discover the things you *don't* know."

"And vice versa." Hallie sat down with her toast and got busy tearing off the crusts, focusing on them instead of me. "Let's start with basics. Do you know what Chronos does?"

"What the world thinks it does, or what it really does?" I asked.

"The world doesn't know about Chronos."

"Mine does."

"The Hourglass?"

I nodded. "For a long time, we just referred to Chronos as *The Powers That Be.* We thought you were like . . . an absentee-landlord governing body. According to Liam, that's what Chronos used to be. Protectors of time. He left when your mom took over, and I guess things changed a lot after that."

"They changed even more when Dad got involved. He didn't think she was making the most of her resources. I can promise governing was the last thing on his mind. Even less so now."

"What is?" I flipped open the top of the honey to pour some on my toast and waited for her to continue.

"Industry. He locates artifacts, artwork, jewelry, etc., and we go get them. Most often, they're related to time, but not always."

I snapped my fingers. "That's how he knew what horology was."

"Dad belongs to at least three different horological societies. Anonymously, of course. Where do you thinks he gets his tips on what to steal?"

"The things he sends you to steal. How does that work?"

"First, I gather intel on the jobs. I learn work schedules, security systems, weakest links, things like that. I do it all by changing my appearance."

"You case joints. Like a burglar." A stray drop of honey landed on the edge of my plate. I slicked my finger over it and licked it off. "And now I'm imagining you in spandex, scaling the side of a building."

Hallie didn't respond. I thought I'd offended her, somehow, but when I looked up, she was staring at my hand. "Hallie?"

"What?" she asked, startled. "Sorry. What did you just say?"

"Um . . . nothing." I put down my toast and wiped my finger on a napkin. "The jobs. Chronos. I thought your dad didn't like for you to leave the house."

"That's where the time gene comes in. I have . . . there's a guy who can teleport. We do jobs together, or we used to. Dad trusted him to make sure I stayed in line. Turns out, trusting him was a stupid choice for both of us."

I tamped down the desire to tell her about Poe. "How?"

"He sided with my mother. She and my dad are still married, even though it's a really weird arrangement. I've seen pictures from their wedding and from when I was a baby. I remember how things used to be. They were either really good actors or they were happy at one point. Sometimes, I think I was nothing more than a phase to her."

"You and your mom aren't close?" I asked.

"Not even in the same galaxy."

Sadness or anger drew down the corners of her mouth. Then I realized it was grief.

"She called me a couple of weeks ago, dropping a bunch of hints, and that's one reason why your revelation at Lafitte's didn't surprise me. I'd heard of the Infinityglass before. I used to get bedtime stories, too."

Another thing we had in common.

"At first, I thought she was just looking for something that Chronos had retrieved. But she used one of the few soft spots I have for her against me, reminding me of the stories, and told me I was the Infinityglass. I wanted to call her a liar, but . . . things have changed for me. Recently. Another reason you didn't surprise me."

"You have symptoms beyond the ripple sightings?" I asked. "Besides the possession?"

She nodded but didn't elaborate. "Any answers I get from her now will have to be bargained for, and it's not worth it."

"She knows what you are, and she won't help you? How could a mother do that?"

"Because she wants something from me." Hallie picked up her

toast. "She always does. I don't know what it is this time, and I don't really want to find out. It won't be good. It won't be loving, or in my best interest. Nothing she does ever is."

"Then don't get answers from her. Get them from me." It was the boldest I'd been about the Infinityglass since the night at Lafitte's.

She exhaled. "I'm ready when you are."

"Then let's take it upstairs."

I put my plate in the sink and exited the kitchen, leaving her with a curious expression and a mouth full of toast.

I set up my laptop, an external drive, and notebook on Hallie's vanity.

It was the first time I'd actually been in her room. A confection of pastels, it was huge and relentlessly neat, with toe shoes hanging from pegs on the wall. I didn't understand why she needed so many different pairs. There were also wigs and tutus.

She had every game system known to man, including a couple of throwbacks, like an Atari console and a Sega Genesis. A tall wooden shelf held hundreds of movies in various forms, Blu-rays, DVDs, even some VHS tapes. I tapped one and raised an eyebrow.

"Not everything has been released in the most modern formats. If you think that's a lot, my digital collection would blow your mind."

"I collect music the way you collect movies." I opened the minimized window on my laptop screen and showed her.

"Seven *thousand* songs?"

"My physical collection would blow *your* mind. It's a sickness. But I like to read, too."

"So do I. Real books. When I was younger, my dad used to take me to the bookstore on Saturdays. Garden District Book Shop at first, but then Octavia Books." Melancholy sneaked into her voice. "I could spend hours in that place; it was so open and full of light. They even had a pet dog that lived in the store. Those were the good old days."

Now when she wanted to leave her house, she had to climb down the side of it.

"Maybe you could take me there sometime."

"Maybe." She shook off the sadness and leaned over my shoulder, her hair swinging forward, so close it brushed against my cheek. "All right, wise one. Enlighten me."

I had two thoughts. One, if I turned my head a fraction of an inch, my lips would line up directly with hers, and two, she knew it.

I scooted the stool closer to the vanity to get myself out of the reach of her lips before clearing my throat.

"Here we go."

Hallie

Dune was easy to tease. The good kind of easy, though. He felt safe and right. I saw how a pattern could form, the push and the pull between us. Not where my brain should be.

"Let's start with the basics," he said, scrolling through a list of documents. "Tell me what you know."

"Right now I'd prefer that you tell me stuff, not that I tell you stuff."

"We both have information." He turned around, too big and too ridiculous, perched on the tiny stool that matched my vanity. "I thought we were going to engage in an *exchange*."

"So you're going to just blindly open up and give me anything I ask for?"

"I don't have time to have trust issues, Hallie, and neither do you."

"There's always time for trust issues."

"If we're going to help each other, we have to put everything on the table." He rubbed his hands on the knees of his jeans and stood. "I've met Poe. Last fall, he came to the Hourglass, to give us an ultimatum from your mom."

"You know Poe?" The admission made me dizzy. "What kind of ultimatum?"

"She wanted us to find someone." His frown told me there was more to the story and that he was weighing whether or not to tell it. "She turned Poe into her sock puppet to get it done, and she claimed it was all for Chronos. She used him."

Not surprising. My mother consistently proved she felt she was entitled to say or do whatever she wanted to get her way. "Who did she want you to find?"

"A man named Jack Landers. She stole a digital storage device called a Skroll, and she needed him to open it."

"What was on it?"

"Information about the Infinityglass," he said. "But the Hourglass stole it from her, and I broke the encryption and downloaded the information on it. When we turned Landers over to your mom, she took the Skroll, but it's missing some info."

I tapped the hard drive that sat on my vanity beside Dune's laptop. "It's all here?"

"That and more. Everything I've gathered over the years, and even some things my dad found before he died."

"My whole life encapsulated in one external drive."

"Not your whole life. Nothing could contain you." The fierceness in his voice surprised both of us.

"I'll take that as a compliment," I said cautiously. "If I want to know what's on that drive, I guess it's my turn in the sharing circle?"

"It's a very small circle."

Small, but suddenly not as cozy as I'd like.

His fingers tapped on his track pad. "Will you talk to me about your . . . symptoms?"

I searched his eyes. Trusted what I saw. "I started seeing rips, but apparently everyone else with the time gene does, too." He nodded confirmation. "My energy levels are insane. I don't need to sleep or eat. I do, out of habit, but it isn't necessary. All my senses feel sharper. And I heal really fast. Insanely fast. I can also hold any form I change into a lot longer. Things like my vocal cords and hair color have always been either impossible or complicated. Not anymore. No effort at all."

"Show me."

I thought for a second, and then morphed into Zoe Saldana à la *Star Trek*.

"James T. Kirk who? Spock who? Bring me a sexy Samoan." I slipped back into my normal skin. "Are you okay? You kind of look like you swallowed your tongue."

"Fine. I'm fine." He rubbed one hand over his face, picked up a pencil, and started scribbling in his spiral notebook.

"The possession, or whatever, isn't connected to my transmutation ability. It's new, part of the Infinityglass thing." I tried to sound casual as I asked the next question. "Do you have a theory on how the Infinityglass part of me kicked into gear?"

He tapped the eraser end of his pencil on the vanity. "It could be . . . hormonal."

"Excuse me?"

"That wasn't meant as any kind of insult; it's just a known trigger for some people. Usually, it's puberty." Dune gave me the once-over, and then started scribbling in his notebook again.

"Yeah. I passed that a long time ago."

"Obviously." He wouldn't look at me. "Or the genetic stressor could be an object or a million other things."

I could tell from his expression and the speed of his pencil on the paper that he was thinking a hundred miles an hour. I was also pretty sure I knew what the trigger was, but I couldn't go there yet. I had to talk to Poe.

"What happened with the rip is another side effect, like your senses or sleeping or energy level. I can't stop thinking about all the variances. For us, back in Ivy Springs, the rips progressed. At first, only travelers could see them, and they could be interacted with. Then they became scenes, and the travelers existed outside them. Then anyone with an active time gene could see rips, whole scenes. Rip worlds. Time started blending: rips with humans but no interaction between the two."

"But I interacted with rip people. Stepped into someone else's life. Has anyone else done that?"

"I don't think so. Here's a list of everything everyone has seen." He leaned back so I could see his computer screen, and then pointed to a desktop folder titled "IG." "I'm going to send you this file. It contains all the basics about the Infinityglass, from when I thought it was an object. If you want to look over it, we can talk about it, see if any of it applies to you."

"You mean, slick as glass, gritty, curvy, immalleable?"

"If those are the ones that work." He shut his laptop and

slipped it into the case. "Have you decided whether or not I'm a nice guy?"

"My only other option for answers is my mother, and I'd trust Darth Maul before I'd trust her."

"You're killing me with the nerd references. But you know that, don't you?"

My phone buzzed with a text from my dad.

The job is on.

I grinned. "The verdict is in, and I think you're a nice guy. You're also my best bet for information about the Infinityglass."

"So we can continue our search tomorrow?" he asked.

My grin got even bigger. "Actually, I have other plans for tomorrow."

Chapter 10
Hallie

I went to the side entrance of the house to wait for Dune.

Because I was excited to see him.

I used to meet Benny at the same entrance when I was a kid. I didn't want to throw a Benny-shaped shadow over Dune, and I didn't think I was. Benny had been my friend. Dune was . . . different.

I wanted to punch myself in my own face. The last thing I needed to indulge in was a crush, especially one that had exploded on me like a shaken champagne bottle.

"Hey, kiddo." Carl, who'd been head of security for as long as I could remember, stood and brushed biscuit crumbs from his shirt. "Is something wrong?"

"Take a load off," I said, briefly placing my hand on his shoulder. "I'm waiting for someone."

"New kid?" He sat, but kept his posture straight and his feet flat on the floor. Ready to jump in front of me at any second, should the need arise.

"We're going on a job."

Carl knew exactly what that meant.

"First one for this guy?" When I nodded, he picked up his Styrofoam cup of hot chocolate and took a slow sip. "And you think he'll be good in the field?"

"We'll find out. All Dune has to do is take a little trip with me."

"To where?"

Dune stepped through the door. Raindrops caught in his black hair, and some settled on the shoulders of his navy windbreaker. He looked mysterious, coming in from the outside mist, kind of like a mystical warrior.

Wow. That cheese stunk like Roquefort.

"The Bourbon Orleans," I said brightly. "One of the oldest hotels in New Orleans. It's also one of the most haunted."

He slid his arms out of his jacket and hung it up on a hook by the door before dropping his bag. "Do you believe in that stuff?"

"I can transmutate. Ghosts don't seem like a stretch."

Dune cast a quick glance over at Carl, who just smiled.

"Bye, Carl," I said, kissing him on the cheek.

"Good luck, and be careful." Carl wiped hot chocolate foam off his upper lip. He was still smiling.

I hooked my arm through Dune's and led him toward the

living room. It was a really nice arm. Strong. Defined. Tan with just a scattering of dark hair.

"You're pretty open about your ability," he said.

"Carl's been around for years. We don't have extended family. Or friends." I wasn't ready to let go of his arm yet, so I guided him toward the stairs and my bedroom. "Dad just hires staff instead."

"You aren't tight with the people you work with?"

"Not really. I'm older than Amelia and Zooey." I wasn't even going to touch the Poe relationship. "Besides that, it's me and my dad, and the guards. Are you tight with the people you work with?"

"The Hourglass operates as a family. Our boss encourages it. You care about people; you have their backs when it comes down to the hard situations. I know how hokey that sounds."

"It doesn't sound hokey at all. Kind of nice, truthfully."

"You're lonely."

He said it in a gentle tone, and it was an observation, not a question, but I felt like I needed to explain. "I have other people besides the ones I work with. There's Gina, my dance teacher. I mean, it's only the two of us, but I see her three days a week. I've taken a couple of classes at the theater where she teaches."

"Dance class and Chronos jobs." He raised his hand, and for a second, I thought he was going to touch my face. My heart caught in my chest, but he scratched his chin instead.

"What? You don't like the way I live my life?"

"You have so much to offer, Hallie. The world needs you like nature needs sunlight."

"That's . . . possibly the sweetest thing anyone has ever said to me."

He answered with a frown.

Feeling too close and too obvious, I pulled away from him. My body went cold without his heat. He rubbed his arm, like he was missing my warmth, too.

Or I was losing my mind, or something worse.

"Anyway, neither of my parents had big families. So it's just us." I walked into my bedroom, looking over my shoulder to see if he'd follow. He hesitated, but he came in. Then I dropped the bomb on him. "How do you feel about staying with me in the hotel this weekend?"

He blinked a couple of times. "Non sequitur much?"

"Sit." I took the tiny vanity stool, partly from guilt that it was so small it barely supported him, and partly because I wanted to see what he looked like on my bed.

"A hotel?"

"Yeah." I did a nervous side to side spin. "For a job. We need to retrieve something from the lobby."

"When your dad hired me, he told me there was a good chance I would end up going on a Chronos job. I think he said many of them were questionable. He never said anything about taking his daughter to a hotel."

"If you want to bail . . ."

"No! No, I don't want to bail."

My slow grin was answered with an immediate blush.

"I mean, I'm going to do the job. You're stuck with me. I just . . . if I'm going to get arrested for a 'retrieval,' I should maybe make arrangements for bail ahead of time."

"No one said anything about stealing. A family donated an antique crystal ball for display, but there was some kind of mix-up, and the hotel got the real thing."

"Were they supposed to get a copy?"

"Yes," I said. "The family needs the original back. They can't waltz in and get it, you see, because they're respectable now, with political aspirations. None of them wants the public to know what kind of value they place on it, or that it tells the truth about the past and shows the promises of the future."

"We're doing a bait and switch, then?"

"Just a switch." I grinned. "You really don't know much about breaking the rules, do you?"

He shook his head.

"Well, then. I look forward to teaching you." I meant it.

Except . . . every time a Chronos job came up I felt torn. There was a constant pull between the desire to get out of my house and do a job well and the need to define myself beyond Chronos and my father's expectations. Dance allowed for that, but only within the boundaries of my studio.

Taking Dune on the Bourbon Orleans job was necessary to keep him on Dad's good side, and to keep him around. While I was the one who suggested he go on the job with me, it had been before he and I had become . . . whatever we were now.

He was the only part of my life that wasn't solely connected to Chronos, and suddenly, I didn't want him to see me in light of what I did there. I didn't want him to forget the Hallie he'd managed to discover over the past couple of weeks.

And I didn't want to forget her either.

The hotel was just off Jackson Square.

We caught a cab instead of using my dad's driver. Maintaining anonymity was a bitch. The rain had cleared out, and the sun was shining. The cabbie dropped us off on the corner of Orleans and Bourbon so we could walk to the main entrance from the side street.

"I brought my computer," Dune said, lifting up his backpack. "Did you look at the file I sent you? If we have time, we could go over it."

I had a vision of us sitting, our heads bent close together, staring at his laptop screen. It progressed to our hands touching accidentally, and then our shoulders, and then . . .

He was looking at me, and I was standing on Bourbon with my mouth hanging open.

"Sure. If we have time." I'd only skimmed it. I pushed my sunglasses up on my head so I could see his eyes. "We'll check in first. I need you to scout the case the crystal ball is in. Make sure it's movable, see if there's a lock, that kind of thing. It's in front of the check-in desk. We'll do some observing, and later, I'll create a diversion in the lobby while you take the crystal."

"If that doesn't work?" he asked.

"Then we'll apply stealth."

"Maybe we should apply it from the get-go." He put his hand at the small of my back, and the valet and the doorman held the double doors open for us. The lobby was full of grandiose furniture, fine art, and huge bouquets of flowers in crystal vases. The blooms smelled absolutely divine.

I sashayed up to the check in desk and plopped down my fake ID and credit card.

"Welcome to the Bourbon Orleans. How may I assist you?"

"Check in. Christian Arnold."

"Yes, miss." Her name tag read OLGA, and I was pretty sure the accent was Norwegian. "Would you like to leave the room on this credit card?"

"I would. And you should have a package for me?"

She frowned. "I don't see a note on the reservation. Just a moment, please. Excuse me."

When she disappeared through a doorway, I pushed Dune away from the desk. "That case. Over there. Just be casual."

I turned back just as Olga came around the corner.

"I'm sorry, Miss Arnold. We didn't have anything for you."

"Oh, let me check my e-mail and make sure I read it correctly." I was trying to give Dune more time, but cut it short when

I realized Olga was doing a thorough job of checking him out. "Never mind. I'll look later."

I stared at her for a couple of seconds before she startled and began flipping through a stack of papers.

"Certainly. And you'll be staying in one of our signature Saint Ann balcony loft suites. I do hope you'll enjoy it. It's very romantic." She shot a look of approval over my shoulder.

"Romantic?" Oh hell. When Dad's assistant had made the original reservation over a month ago, she'd counted on me being in the hotel alone, and Poe popping in and out. No need for two rooms or for two beds. "Do you have anything else?"

"We're booked for the weekend, but the suite is one of our nicest. I'm sure it will meet your expectations." I turned to see that she was focusing on Dune, who was leaning intently toward the glass case and talking to a hotel employee, while *pointing to the crystal on the top shelf.*

"I'm sure it will be lovely. Where's the elevator?" I asked with forced cheer.

Olga pointed. "Right that way."

I gave her a smile that displayed all my teeth, then spun on one high heel and approached Dune, grabbing his arms and dragging him away from the case.

"Thanks for the info," Dune called out over his shoulder to the bellman.

"Enjoy your stay," the bellman said back, tipping his cap.

"I'm sure I will."

"I wouldn't count on it," I muttered, squeezing his elbow and steering him toward the elevator.

Dune

"You don't have to squeeze so hard." I stifled a yelp. "Or pinch."

Hallie pinched me again, I guess for good measure. "Could you have been any more obvious?"

"There was a plaque with tiny, tiny print that covered the occult in Victorian times, and information on the *plaçage*. And some other stuff." I gulped at the scary-angry look on her face. "I'm a reader. I was reading. It gave me a good excuse to ask the bellman questions."

According to the plaque, the Bourbon Orleans had lived through many incarnations, starting as the home to the Orleans Ballroom in 1817. It had seen masquerades, carnival balls, and quadroon balls, and then turned into a convent and a school. In 1964, it became a hotel, with a reputation for excellent service and numerous hauntings.

From the orphan children who'd suffered through the yellow fever epidemic to a Civil War soldier to a dancer who whirled under the ballroom chandelier, there was a promising possibility of ghosts, or a terrifying rip or two.

"You didn't need to ask questions. You were talking to an employee about the thing we are planning on stealing."

"You said we were retrieving, not stealing."

She pinched me again as we got on the elevator.

"You're bossy," I said. "Maybe a little bit mean."

"It's like you forgot why we were here."

"Maybe I was a little thrown off when I overheard that we're staying in the 'romantic' loft suite." Or a lot thrown off.

The elevator doors dinged open. "It just worked out that way. Don't worry, Saint Dune, I don't plan on compromising your integrity."

"No, of course not, because stealing has nothing to do with integrity." The words were a whisper, but they echoed down the hallway.

"Retrieval," Hallie said through gritted teeth as she pushed me inside the suite. "Here's an idea. Try not to blow it all before we even get started. And I told you, we're not . . . whoa."

A red leather couch was backed up to an exposed brick wall. Across from it sat a small desk and a huge flat screen. The room was perfectly proportioned. French doors opened onto a private balcony, or gallery, as they are called in Lousiana. A split staircase led upstairs. To the bedroom.

Where there was one bed. One big, big bed and a bottle of champagne.

"I'll take the couch," I said. Or better yet, we'd finish the job today, and I would go home, lock myself in my apartment, and stand in a cold shower for two solid days.

"Don't be passive-aggressive." She threw her bag on the desk, unzipped it, and pulled out a sweater. "We can share the same breathing space for a day. Screw this job up and get me in trouble, and I'll be forced to find inventive ways to injure your man parts."

I tried to hide my smile as I sat down on the couch. Everything with Hallie was easy and complicated at the same time, in the very best way, but being alone with her in a hotel room with one bed was one complication I had no idea how to handle.

"Maybe you just want to think about my man parts." Apparently I was going to handle it overtly.

She blinked a couple of times. Finally. I'd managed to throw her off. "Maybe I should do this myself."

"I said I was in. I'm supposed to be helping you."

"Right. Because you were so helpful in the lobby?"

"We both know you could do this job blindfolded in a blackout," I argued. "Just like I know why you want to be here."

"I don't think you do."

"You wanted out of your house," I said. "You're out. What else is there?"

Her look of frustration told me there was a lot more. "Maybe I wanted to get somewhere private and give you a chance to kiss me."

I almost fell out of my seat. Her excuse was a diversion from the truth, and the perfect one to throw at me. I stood.

Tilting her head up, she moved close enough that our chests were almost touching. "Hallie," I warned.

"Don't you want to?"

"Want to what?"

Her hands went to her hips. "Kiss me."

Caution spun my brain dry. "Not a good idea."

"Not good," she agreed. *"Great."*

"It isn't—"

"We're alone. Legitimately alone. Hint. There's . . . tension, and maybe I'd like to ease it. What's the problem?"

"Too fast. Out of nowhere. Complications. Cloudy motives."

"All I see is sunshine."

I couldn't give in for a few reasons. One was fear of an imminent explosion. Another was that I was obviously outmatched, and I didn't know how I'd make myself stop kissing her if I ever started.

"Listen." I took a huge step back. Breathed. Breathed again. In that moment, honesty outweighed sense. "I'm not going to pretend like this isn't something I want. You're amazing."

"Okay." She looked confused.

"I thought you should know."

"You're either feeling sorry for me or buttering me up, and only one of those options makes sense."

"It's neither."

"Okay, then," she said. "I'm amazing. Know what else is amazing? My kissing. Are you going to find out or not?"

"No." I backed up another step. "Because you're frustrated, and I don't know if I'm the cause or the cure."

"Maybe you're both."

"Maybe that's not good enough for me."

"Oh my damn." She dropped her head into her hands. "A guy with standards."

"A guy who likes you." It was out before I could pull it back.

She jerked her head up. "You like me?"

I didn't answer.

"I can't do this right now. I'm sorry I . . . tried to jump you, or whatever." She picked up her bag. "Let's just get the job done, and then I'll . . . I don't know what."

Before I could say another word, she disappeared into the bathroom. I went to the bedroom and changed into my suit, then came back down to wait. When she opened the door fifteen minutes later, I lost all feeling in my extremities.

"I . . . you." I cleared my throat. "It . . . um. Hi."

"Hi." The fire had mellowed, but I could still feel it. "Does this work?"

The shirt wasn't low cut or black, but dark blue. It shimmered, and covered her from collarbone to hip bone. Classy.

But when she did a slow spin, a cutout showed off most of her bare back, the one that had started haunting my waking moments as well as my dreams.

"It works."

The tie on my suit had barely been snug, but now it was

insanely tight. Maybe I needed to compliment her. Girls usually responded well to compliments. I had no idea what the protocol was for intended theft or retrieval.

"That shirt is like . . . a mullet. Business in the front, party in the back."

"That is an absolutely terrible comparison."

I swallowed really hard. "It was supposed to be a compliment."

"You don't date much, do you?"

I stared at her, unsure of what to do next. "Do you need a jacket or something?"

"And mess up the look?" She batted her eyelashes dramatically.

Definitely didn't want to mess up the look. "I'll give you mine if you get cold."

"No, you leave your jacket on. Any bodyguard worth his salt is going to be carrying."

"I don't have a weapon. I don't need one."

"I realize that you're He-Man sized and all, but your role in this little drama is to act as my bodyguard. If something bad goes down and you aren't armed, we're both in trouble." She sighed, dug around in her bag, and shoved a stun gun into my hands.

I stared at it. "I have no idea what to even do with this thing."

"Just make sure the safety's on so you don't tase your nuts off."

As I often found with Hallie, I had no idea how to respond.

"I'm not going to lie and say that most often I find it disgusting when men can't look above my shoulders. But above my shoulders is where you usually look."

"That's where your eyes are." I sounded like an idiot.

"Do you know anyone who has eyes elsewhere?"

"I mean that's where your intelligence is. I can see it there. I like that part of you."

"I know. And that might be where your focus is right now, but I have to be honest. After our earlier conversation, I'm hoping your thoughts are somewhere else entirely."

Chapter 11

Hallie

I needed to be 100 percent to do a job, and I had to do this one well to keep Dune in my father's employ. Now he had my thoughts spinning, and other parts of me aching. We were alone in a hotel. I'd thought there was something happening between us beyond a working relationship, but I couldn't even convince him to stray a smidge into moral ambiguity. All he could think about was the job. I just wanted a kiss. So I would have an answer.

Not that I knew the question.

"Ready?" Dune asked.

"Unless you've changed your mind about the kissing."

He put his hand on the doorknob.

"Fine. Now is the perfect time to go down, anyway. People will be leaving for dinner, checking in, and there's some sort of reception in the lobby."

"Why do you want more people instead of less people?

Shouldn't you wait until the dead of night?"

"No." I checked my lipstick one more time in the mirror, and caught Dune checking out my bare back. "Too much security camera action if we do it that way."

"Why does that matter? You can change your appearance." He picked up the key card and dropped it into his pocket.

"Right. But you can't. If you were Poe, this would've been simpler."

"I'm sorry to disappoint." He sounded so touchy I had to grin.

"I didn't mean it that way, and you know it."

We took the guest elevator to the second floor and wandered down the hall until we found the staff elevator. We needed to take it to the lobby so we could enter from the back.

"I like being with you," I said. "I like you in general. I wasn't trying to be insensitive. I was merely speaking truth, and as previously discussed, I can show you how not disappointed I will be later. If we get through this without any incidents."

When the elevator doors closed behind us, I gave into my urge, turned to face him, and traced one finger along his jaw line.

His expression was stoic. "If you want to avoid an incident, you should probably not touch me."

"But that's the kind of incident I could get into."

"Hallie." He grabbed my fingers and lowered our joined hands.

"Saved by the elevator," I said as the doors opened.

The lobby was hopping. A few businessmen, a couple of families, and a trio of transvestites all gathered around the piano in the corner. The man behind it played "When the Saints Go Marching In" at a roaring clip. I shook my head in disgust.

"People feed off stereotypes in the Quarter, and we grow them like algae. When I see things like that, I wonder if it's the irony of the locals or the idiocy of the infiltrators. Plus, it's a little hard to cause a distraction when there's a sing-along happening."

"You could get on top of the piano," he said, without missing a beat.

I laughed, a real one. Dune could pull them out of me like magic. "We can wait until it's a little calmer."

"Nope." He unbuttoned his suit jacket. I glanced at his pants pocket to see if I could make out the Taser, but realized too late that it totally looked like I was checking out his assets.

"I was making sure you had your weapon," I blurted out when he raised his eyebrows.

He grinned.

"I was looking for the Taser in your pants." When he snort laughed, I closed my eyes and shook my head. "Oh hell, can we just get out of here?"

"I said no. I have an idea. Do you have the replacement crystal in your purse?"

I nodded.

"Go stand by the case and get ready to make a move."

"Excuse me?" I put my hands on my hips. "Did you just try to boss me on a job I brought you on?"

"I see a way to solve the problem right now. Trust me."

He turned and walked away, did a check of the lobby, and then stared at the largest vase of flowers.

It took me a minute to figure out what he was doing, and another ten seconds to figure out it was going to work. I took off for the display case.

Every vase in the lobby started to wobble back and forth—the ones at the entrance, on the piano, on the check-in desk, and on every table. The next wave of movement touched the vases in the niches on the walls, and on each table in the restaurant. Finally, the giant water dispenser with fresh-cut lemons and limes started to slosh its contents furiously back and forth.

And then they all crashed to the ground at once.

I switched the crystals in fifteen seconds easy, and turned back to the lobby.

The people around the piano were jumping around, trying to keep their feet out of the puddles. "Was that an earthquake? Does New Orleans have earthquakes?"

"My suitcase is soaking wet!" A woman at the check-in desk looked like she expected the trusty Olga to suck the excess water up with her mouth, while Olga ran for an armful of cloth napkins.

Dune stood smiling, as chaos reigned. Then he met my eyes.

He crossed the lobby and took my hand.

I followed him up a staircase to a couch on a landing, nerves swirling. The sounds from the lobby echoed up to us, but otherwise the quiet was heavy.

"What's going on?" he asked, sitting down.

"You've worked for Chronos for five minutes, and you figure out how to do a job on the fly. I was going to cop out because of a sing-along."

Dune's emotions were controlled, while mine were bouncing off the inside of my chest like a rubber ball.

"Did I make you angry by going off plan?"

"No."

"You have the crystal ball, isn't that all that matters?"

"No, I'm just . . . I don't . . . this is *my* thing, not your thing. The Hourglass doesn't steal."

"Retrieve." He grinned and pulled me down beside him. Close beside him. "You're acting like doing jobs for Chronos is the only thing that defines you."

I rubbed the skin above my sternum and wondered if I was too young for a heart attack. "It feels like it is. Like it always will. I'll have to be the one to take it over, the one to carry it into the next generation, whether I want to or not. I'll inherit all my parents' choices, and more seclusion, more bodyguards, more attempts on my life. All that good stuff. I look at my life and the only thing I see in front of me is Chronos."

"I don't think that's true, Hallie. It doesn't have to be that way."

"You want to know why I think my mom is such an unfortunate human? She has the lamest ability ever."

He took my hand away from my heart, held it.

"She's a human clock. Ask her what time it is. She knows it to the second. It was fun when I was little, but the novelty wore off. I think she resents what I can do. The point is, she made up for her lack of ability by taking over. Having the most power. Wielding it over me. I don't want to be her. I don't want Chronos to define me. Ever."

"Tell me what you want."

"To go to Newcomb. They have an amazing dance program. And then I'd dance professionally, anywhere—it doesn't need to be prestigious—and truthfully, I want to stay in New Orleans. There's so much art here, and so much room to create all kinds of things. Not that I've seen much of it in person lately. But I know what the nightlife is like in the Quarter, and I remember all the performance art in the square." I hadn't set foot in it since Benny died. I could barely manage seeing the statue of Andrew Jackson along the skyline if I glimpsed it from a side street. "This city breathes, and I'm oxygen starved."

"Then do it."

"That's the problem," I said. "I can't."

Dune

"You'll find a way."

"What makes you so sure?" Hallie asked.

"Because . . . you're challenging." I paused to rephrase when she frowned. "Let me explain. Poe told me before I met you that you were smart. A genius. That's true."

"What else did he tell you?"

"That you were . . . ah . . . sexy."

She pulled her hand away and her eyes went wide. "Did he—"

"He told me that whatever happened between you didn't work out, and that he cares about you and considers you to be one of his best friends. That's all I need to know."

"Oh. Okay. I didn't realize you were that close," she said.

"It was a debriefing." I kept going, hoping she wouldn't dig deeper into my connection with Poe. "He also told me that you know what you want and how to get it. I haven't seen anything that tells me differently. Whatever you decide to do with your life, you'll do."

"You're one of the few who knows non-Chronos Hallie. I was frustrated upstairs, and I'm sorry I took it out on you. But you need to know that I like you." She lifted her hands and let them flutter to her lap. "I think . . . you're solid. You're pretty. In a very manly way, of course."

"Have you noticed how often you render me speechless?"

"It's not purposeful, I swear. My brain overloads my senses sometimes."

"I have a friend who says her edit button is broken."

"I never installed mine." She smiled.

"If you like me, why were you so . . . combative today?"

She exhaled. "Because I'm pretty sure you like girls, and I keep flirting with you, and so far, you've responded with a really, really terrible *mullet* reference and those nice things you said a minute ago. But you could have said those in friendship."

"I said them because I believe them. I'm trying to keep things friendly because my purpose is to help you find out what being the Infinityglass means. But . . ."

"But?" She sounded hopeful.

I wanted to kiss her. I wanted to take her face in my hands, thread my fingers through her hair, and kiss her until neither one of us could see or breathe or worry about what was coming next. Then I wanted to go back to the room and . . . yeah.

"But maybe my purpose has skewed a little."

"Why did the Hourglass send you?" She looked up into my eyes. "Why not someone else?"

"My knowledge base is broadest." I was quiet for a minute. "And I'm glad, because I wouldn't want anyone to be here but me."

"Why?" She leaned in, and her eyes were on my lips.

"Because I wouldn't have met you. The Infinityglass would've been cold and impersonal to me, and I needed it to have a face."

Because now that it did, everything had changed.

"I'm glad you're here, too." She stopped for a moment, thinking. "What you did in the lobby was so *amazing*. I know you don't like to use it, but you can control it."

"Just the small things."

"Then you practice with the big things. It's a gift, Dune, not something you can shove in between your mattress and box spring like a diary. You can't lock it up and forget about it. There could come a time when you need it."

I ran my thumb over the smooth skin on top of her hand. "I'm afraid of losing control. The very last thing I'd ever want to do is hurt someone, even a stranger."

"I understand control. I never feel like I have it, except when I dance."

"I wish I could see you." I pressed my lips together right after I said it. "I mean . . ."

"The Samoan boy blushes. You want to see me dance?"

I searched her face. "I do."

She nodded slowly. "Then follow me."

From the landing where we sat, I followed her up to the second-story lobby. A tapestry hung on one wall above a huge wooden cabinet. Ornate golden carvings on the door displayed a roaring lion with a flowing mane. The more I looked at it, the more it seemed to be a warrior wearing a mask. Two sets of double doors were across from it.

"Locked." Hallie looked around before stepping in front of the lock. I heard a *swish* and then a little *click* as she pulled one of the doors open.

"What did you do?"

"You don't want to know." She tucked her hand in her pocket. "Come on."

She let the door close behind us, and we stood in silence as I took it all in.

A ballroom. A row of windows dressed in golden velvet draperies was divided by a small, simple staircase with four steps. The late afternoon sunlight blurred the edges of a windowed doorway that led to a wide gallery overlooking Orleans Street.

Hallie couldn't take her eyes away from the chandelier hanging in the center of the room.

"Are you going to stare, or dance?" I asked.

"Only if I dance with you."

"That wasn't part of the deal." I felt a little hectic.

"If you want to see me dance, I'm going to do it in your arms."

"Too shy to dance by yourself?" I said. "Afraid, maybe?"

"No. Why?" She raised one eyebrow. "Are you going to double-dog dare me?"

"If I have to."

"Dance is personal." Hallie always had excellent posture, but when she straightened her spine and squared her shoulders, the dancer in her took over. Breathtakingly beautiful. "It's the only time I get to be free. I don't perform very often, and a cage or a stage in a dance club doesn't count."

"You . . . wear clothes when you do that?"

"You're really dropping judgment on me right now?" She knew I was teasing. I could tell by her smile.

"No. I'm doing everything in my power not to picture it."

"I don't believe you."

"You should," I said. "I could pass out. That would be embarrassing."

"You're a terrible tease."

"I know. I'm not sure how to approach this." I'd have been more comfortable trying to figure out how to hack into the pope's e-mail.

"You can start by shutting up and putting your arms around me. Take my hand in yours. Put the other one on the small of my back."

"According to online surveys, the small of a woman's back is one of the places she most wants to be touched."

"You touch me there all the time. Do you read a lot of surveys about where women like to be touched?"

"Um."

"Where are some of the other places?" She met my eyes dead on. "If you think I'm going to let this go, you're so, so wrong."

"Clavicle."

"And?"

"Crooks of elbows. Backs of knees. Nape of neck."

"You're leaving out some really obvi—"

"Hallie?"

She grinned and batted her lashes. "Yes."

"Maybe we should just dance." My palm met hers while my other hand settled on her waist.

There was a subtle, slight hitch in her breathing.

"Your breath just caught." I said it without thinking.

"Maybe it did. So what?" She angled her chin up at me.

"Nothing. It's just . . . it's only fair. You make mine catch all the time."

Chapter 12
Hallie

I'd never swooned in my life.

But if Dune kept talking sweet to me, I was going to need a fainting couch and smelling salts pronto.

His touch was gentle, and he smelled like the ocean. Not fishy ocean, but expensive, man-made, bottled interpretation of the ocean. I couldn't believe how nervous I was in his arms, or how overwhelmed I was by my emotions when he pulled me closer.

Then the world melted around us.

Rivulets of the past flooded over the present, and the song playing in my mind bloomed from a few simple notes to a full orchestra. What I thought would be a waltz became a quadrille. Dune's face faded. A masquerade mask replaced it, and the rip world replaced my own.

The eyes behind the satin assess me from head to toe. A cool expression turns warm as what he sees passes muster. When the time comes to switch partners, he pulls me from formation.

"Cecile?"

I nod.

"You look beautiful. The dress pleases you?"

I nod again and offer a tentative smile.

"I'm going to arrange a meeting with your mother. Does this please you, too?"

"Monsieur Brionne." My maman *interrupts us. She wears a yellow dress of a much brighter shade than my own. Both complementary of our dark hair and skin. My skin and . . .*

. . . not my skin. I looked down at my fingernails, not recognizing the oval shapes and bitten nails. I didn't bite my nails.

"May I call upon Cecile tomorrow?" Monsieur Brionne asks my maman. *He keeps his hand at my waist, and I know that he doesn't want to let me go. Something about the way his fingers grip my waist is worrisome; as is the look in his eyes that tells me he hopes I'll be alone tomorrow when he calls.*

"That will be agreeable." Maman dips her head into a slight bow.

The music begins, slow and disarming, and we step back into the throng of dancers, everyone here is part of the system of plaçage, arranged left-handed marriages of prosperous white men and women of color.

The soft glow of an electric chandelier replaces candlelight, and the smell of calla lilies perfumes the air as bodies whirl around me.

Monsieur Brionne stops, and I spin out of his arms. The room fades, tilts, and the light changes, going from soft focus to sharp relief.

"A joining of two fine families." I jump when a man with a shiny, bald head claps me on the shoulder. "Congratulations."

"Thank you."

I didn't recognize my own voice.

My dress was no longer yellow, but stark white, and my hair fell in blond ringlets below my shoulders. A huge diamond graced my left ring finger, with a gold band below it.

"I'm so happy."

The words came out of my mouth and not my mouth. The kiss I received landed softly on my cheek and not my cheek.

"No happier than I."

I knew this man would be gentle, unlike Monsieur Brionne. He looked at me with the same kindness Dune did.

Dune.

"David." I hold his hand as my new husband guides me across the crowded room. He takes two champagne glasses from a tray, and gives one to me.

"To my bride," he says. "To Melina."

"To Melina," the crowd says in chorus.

Before I could catch my breath, the scene changed again.

Six women in prayer. A rosary in my hand. My hair in a tight bun. Feelings of peace, concern, benevolence. And sensible shoes.

The yellow fever is spreading; bodies lie in piles on the streets outside. We can't take on any more orphans, but the infection makes new ones every day. Every hour.

Is it punishment? Justice? Crying, hungry children speak of neither.

The sound of a bouncing ball echoes down the hallway. Playtime and prayer time blend into an ache in my chest.

The ache spread out through my limbs, and my head began to spin. Three sets of sight competed, fighting for purchase.

Maman and I, leaving the ballroom as Monsieur Brionne watches.

My husband and I, laughing as we dance in the middle of the floor.

My gnarled hands and the pain in my knees, speaking of good use and great age as I kneel to pray.

"Hallie."

Who is Hallie?

"Please, Hallie. Wake up."

I squeezed my eyes closed, breathed deeply into my center, and pushed.

Cecile Dupart.

Melina Landrieu.

Sister Mary Christina.

Their worlds disappeared, but their memories remained. Time sealed itself shut behind them, and the ballroom fell silent.

I'd experienced more life than I could ever live on my own in the Bourbon Orleans ballroom, in the span of a few seconds. Something in me sensed the wrongness of the situation, but that didn't mean I didn't want it. I could go on a thousand jobs for Chronos, but I'd never dance in a pre–Civil War ballroom. I could fall in love a hundred times, but I'd never be the debutante who married an aspiring politician in the calm that came before the Vietnam War. I could live for eighty more years, but I'd never, ever be a nun.

Ever.

"Hallie?"

My eyes flew open. It took me a few seconds to focus on the chandelier above me, and a few more to find Dune's gray green eyes.

"Dune?" I was on the floor. "What happened?"

"I don't think we should talk about this here." His face was drawn, his eyes guarded.

"Why?" I struggled to sit.

"Not here, Hallie."

He scooped me up in his arms like I weighed nothing. I rested my head on his chest, barely noticing my surroundings as he took me to the room.

The unfamiliar memories that now belonged to me repeated

on playback in my brain. I had real power. Not false bravery or blustering confidence. I could still feel it in my veins, pulsing under my skin.

"Are you okay?" Dune sat beside me so softly that the couch barely moved, a feat for someone his size. He brushed my hair back from my face.

How had we gotten to the room so quickly?

"I don't know." I tried to sit up and he helped me, his arm around my waist. "Was . . . was it like last time?"

"It was different." Caution kept his voice guarded. "Powerful."

"It felt like freedom. Ultimate, supernatural freedom. I lived other people's lives through their eyes, and I felt all their emotions. But you didn't feel that, did you? What did you see?"

He didn't answer. Just looked at me like he was afraid of me.

"Dune?"

"You changed."

Dune

"You were three different people. At first, you just froze. Your face was expressionless." Her irises had reflected the light pouring in through the windows, and she'd stopped blinking. I'd stepped back from her, and that's when her feet left the ground. "Then the rip sucked you in. It was all around me, but I wasn't part of it."

Like I was the ghost, and the rip world was the reality.

"What else?" she prompted.

"Your facial features rearranged. When it happened outside Lafitte's, it was one face. Today, it was three. A young girl with brown eyes. A blonde with a slightly crooked nose. An older woman with dark skin. You were three people in quick succession, and then, somehow, you were all three at once."

She nodded and let out a shaky breath. "Sounds about right."

"You pushed them back. The images from the room flowed into the hole in time, and the rips went in, too. And you were back."

She was shaking so hard her teeth chattered.

"Hallie, look at me. You're either cold or in shock. Let's get you into something more comfortable."

When she didn't take advantage of the tease I'd set up, my stomach dropped. I grabbed her bag, unzipped it, and handed it over. She fished out a change of clothes, along with her brush and a makeup bag.

"Do you need help with anything?"

"No. Just . . . don't move." She disappeared into the bathroom. I heard running water and an electric toothbrush. A few moments later, she opened the door, wearing yoga pants and a tank top. Her face was clean, and she'd tied her hair in a knot on top of her head.

She picked up her sweater and slid her arms in. She sounded like she'd been screaming for hours. "You're a good baby-sitter."

"I wanted to make sure you were okay."

"I was the Infinityglass, Dune." She curled up on the couch, pulled the sleeves of her sweater down over her hands. "I made the rips go away. I sent them back. That has to be good, right?"

"I don't know." She'd floated and I'd watched the power pulsing through her. Nothing about it felt good. "It was a manifestation of the Infinityglass power. It overtook you, Hallie."

"Then I'll just figure out how to control it. Next time, I'll know what to expect." She dropped her head into her hands. "You're looking at me like I scared you."

"I'm scared for you. I know that letting me take care of you right now would be harder than taking care of yourself." I touched her knee. "But . . ."

She looked up.

"Let me?" I asked.

I got my answer when she crawled into my arms.

Once she was asleep, I carried her to the bed and stepped out onto the gallery.

It was dark, and a mist hung just above the street. It was the quietest I'd ever heard New Orleans, but even the loudest couldn't compete with the noise in my head. I used my phone to send an e-mail detailing what had happened in the ballroom. Then I sat down to wait, searching for the setting sun on the horizon.

Michael didn't e-mail back. He called.

"When did you fall for her?" It was the first thing he said after I answered.

I couldn't deny the relief. Out of everyone, I knew he'd understand.

"I don't know. Immediately?" I exhaled. "All those years obsessing over the Infinityglass, all the things I'd read, so much of it has transferred to her. But, Mike, tonight . . . for a few minutes, I didn't know which Hallie I was seeing. I didn't know if she was there at all."

He was silent for a minute, gathering his thoughts. "No one here has been possessed, and no one can send the rips back. So far, she's the only one."

"So it's an Infinityglass thing."

"I think so."

"Time closed behind her. It healed itself. What if she could send all the rips back? Would it fix things?"

"At this point, the continuum is so compromised there are probably rips all over the world," Michael said. "Definitely too many to keep them balanced by herself."

"She changed. Her body language and her voice." Her essence.

"I still believe she's our answer, Dune, somehow. No idea how it's going to play out, but she's going to change everything."

"If that's true"—I steadied myself to ask the next question— "do you think she can survive it?"

"I don't know." Michael paused for a few seconds before he spoke again. "But I'll help you figure it out. How would you feel about a visit from some friends?"

Chapter 13
Hallie

When I woke up, it was dark.

"Dune?" I was in the hotel bed, alone. And I needed him.

"Yes." His answer was immediate. "Are you okay?"

A small lamp on the far side of the room switched on. He must have been sitting on the stairs. Even though his hair was short, it was messy, like he'd had his hands in it. Worry had threaded itself into the fiber of his being.

"Sit with me?" I asked.

He sat on the side of the bed, I reached out to take his hand.

"Actually . . ." I pulled all the walls down. "Would you hold me?"

He climbed in beside me and gathered me up like he'd been waiting to do it for a lifetime. I let go of everything—nerves, uncertainty, and a disturbing slice of shame—and let him see my fear.

"How long have I been asleep?"

"A couple of hours," he said, smoothing my hair back. It hung loose, having worked itself out of the knot while I slept. "I kept checking on you. You were restless. I was worried. Tell me what to do to make it better."

"We've had this conversation, Obi-Wan. I don't need you to save me." He tensed up, the muscles in his chest and arms going hard. "But I want you to help me."

"Anything you want."

"I need you to know something. I play around, I tease. It's fun." I met his gaze in the faint light. His eyes, usually so full of sweetness, were shielding his emotions. "This? Isn't like that."

"I'm glad."

"When you look at me," I asked, "do you see me, or do you see the Infinityglass? Object or human? I have to know if you see me."

I needed him to see me.

"I spend half of every second making sure I'm separating you from it." His hand brushed across my cheek, surprising us both. He didn't pull it away. "After what happened in that ballroom, I realized I can't take on Hallie the human and leave half of her behind. Because I'm not interested in the things the Infinityglass loves or hates, and I'm done with trying to figure out every single thing about it, when I really want to know about you. To think about you. About kissing you. All the places I want to touch you."

I'd never been paralyzed like this, torn between throwing myself at him and running hard as hell.

"But I was right, earlier," I said. "You're afraid of me."

"I've been afraid of you since I laid eyes on you. Maybe since I heard about you," he said. "That goes way back, Hal. I'm taking on more than a girl."

His hand was still on my face. I reached up and pressed mine on top of it.

"Tell me something, and I need the truth. Do you see me? Or are you interested because I'm there?"

I heard the vulnerability in his voice, and I knew the answer because I'd asked myself the same question.

"I see you, Dune. And I . . . I know. I just . . . I love how . . . honest and . . . thoughtful you are." I couldn't make the words come out the way I wanted. I tangled our fingers together. "You always seem to consider all the angles. You never rush into anything."

So much control.

He managed to frown and look happy at the same time. "If we take this where it seems naturally inclined to go, it's going to make every step that much harder."

"I think it could be worth it."

"I know it could," he said.

Where had he come from? How long would he stay? "Will you go back to the Hourglass when this is over?"

"I don't know. What will you do?"

Hopefully be alive. Anxiety trickled between my shoulder blades like ice water.

"I want the same things I've always wanted. We're talking about you. I don't even know your life plan. What is it?"

"College. My professors let me take my finals early so I could come here."

"Come here and help me?" I put my arm across his stomach and squeezed him. "How is any of this fair to you?"

"Everything I did was my choice. All I have under my belt are core classes. Pretty sure most of those will transfer. I can get into any school I want. Can probably get scholarships, too, at least for undergrad work."

"You want to go to grad school?"

"I'm not counting it out. Loyola has a computer science program, and a newer one in digital humanities that's fascinating."

A spark of hope lit up my chest and shot out to my fingers and toes. "Did you know that before you met me?"

He grinned.

"No."

Dune

Her smile made promises. At least I'd die happy.

"You gave me a list of places women like to be touched." The light was in her eyes again. "Think you can conjure that up about now?"

I took her hand and flipped it over. "Palm."

"Are you going to read it? Because there are palm readers all over Jackson Square. We can go down later and check with a professional."

I drew my index finger down the middle of it and kept going. "Wrist. Inner elbow."

"Oh. That'll work."

Watching her eyes go wide gave me a boost. When I reached her collarbone, I traced it with two fingers. "Clavicle."

"That sounds too scientific. And sharp." A tremble worked its way into her voice.

"Hollow of the throat. Nape of the neck. Shoulder muscles." I massaged some of her tension away, and then brought it all back when I put my hand on the small of her back and pulled her closer. She inhaled sharply when my lips grazed her earlobe.

"You skipped a few."

"We aren't ready for those," I said.

"I'm okay with concentrating on everything you listed."

"You're breathing really fast."

"Is that a scientific observation?" she asked. "Should I make a note?"

"No." I couldn't wait another second. I leaned in.

She kept her lips still when mine touched hers, and I froze, wondering if I'd somehow misread her. I started to pull away.

"No, don't." She held me tighter, sliding over so her body was flush against mine. "I always want to remember what it felt like the first time you touched me. Like this."

"I have a green light, then?" Because now that we were finally here, holding back might kill me.

"It's fluorescent. Blinking. Spinning."

I went slowly, partly because I wanted to drive her crazy, and partly because I wanted to remember the first time I touched her, too.

Her lips, cheeks, eyelids, all got equal attention. Her temples, the spot just below her ear, the hollow of her throat. I traced the length of her spine and slipped my fingertips inside the back of her sweater to feel the skin I'd been dreaming of, loving the catch of her breath. She was as soft and warm as I'd thought she'd be. Better.

Our first kiss was unbearably gentle, considering what I wanted, but I had a point to prove. So much of her life had been fast, lived out in spurts of freedom. I didn't want what we shared to be like anything else she'd ever experienced. Time was compressed, trouble was going down, but I wanted to be part of a long chain of Hallie's memories, which meant I'd be intentional about making them.

She had other ideas.

"My turn," she said, rolling me onto my back. Her hair spilled over her shoulders and tickled my cheeks.

"You're going to wreck my self-control." And my lack of it was a little too obvious.

Leaning forward, she rested her forearms on my chest, touched her lips to mine, and whispered, "That's the goal, yes."

I'd wanted to be close to her, and now I was all kinds of tangled up. I threaded my fingers in her hair, pulled her face closer. "Maybe we should move down to the co—"

"Don't you dare." She trailed her fingertips down to my neck. "I haven't read any surveys about where men like to be touched, but I bet the list is short."

"Only for those who don't want to enjoy the journey."

"You have a way with the sweet talk, Mr. Ta'ala. Don't tell me you're going to be a gentleman."

"That prim and proper expression you're trying on only makes me want to show you what a gentleman I'm not," I teased.

Prim and proper disappeared, and naughty and mischievous took their place.

Heaven help me.

"How about this? I want you to be Hallie the girl. I want to be Dune the boy. I want to kiss you until the sun comes up, and then until the moon rises again. Why should we hurry?"

I knew there could be valid reasons, but I couldn't give in to them. Not yet.

"There's some kind of crazy role reversal going on here." She scraped her teeth across the scruff on my chin. "Aren't you supposed to be trying to talk me into things?"

"We can talk each other into things. Later."

"I'll hold you to that," she said, and then her lips were on mine again.

Chapter 14
Hallie

I rolled over to look at the clock. "It's six A.M."

"I don't want to leave." Dune propped his head on one hand and traced the outline of my bottom lip with the other.

"We could run away."

I looked for the smile in his eyes, but all they told me was that there was too much to run away from. He cupped my cheek and kissed me again.

It was so easy to sink into his body, to fit it to mine, to take the warmth that was an intrinsic part of him. I felt like I'd known him for years, but every touch reduced me to a pile of first-kiss butterflies.

"I have an idea." I pulled away, reluctantly, and tugged at his arm. "Come on."

"Should I be worried?" He rolled his big body off the bed and helped me up.

"Always." I grabbed my sneakers out of my bag, contemplated how they'd look with my yoga pants, and decided I didn't care. "My dad is gone until tonight, and I want to take advantage of that while I can. Can we go back to your place?"

"I need to talk to you about that."

Serious tone. Frown. Uh-oh.

"I live in the Georgian."

"I know the building. That's where Poe lives." Not that I'd ever been inside. He'd just popped into my place when we spent time together.

"Yeah. I live with him."

"*He's back?* How long has he been back?"

"Since I got here. I'm sorry I didn't tell you, but Liam and your dad are trying to keep him off your mom's radar. That's why he hasn't been in touch with you."

I couldn't accuse Dune of lying to me, because I'd never asked where he lived. He'd told me he'd met Poe, even that he'd talked to him about me. I wondered what exactly Poe had told Dune about us, but then dismissed the worry. Poe didn't kiss and tell.

Dune was eyeing me, waiting for an explosion of anger.

"I'm not mad. Mad is a waste of energy. I wanted to go to your place to see it, to draw out my time with you, but Poe and I have some things to discuss. Namely, what the hell he was thinking when he threw in with my mother. How's that going to sit with you?"

"Fine." He rocked back on his heels. "I have some ideas about drawing out my time with you, too."

The statement should've sounded sexy, but instead, it was serious.

"Okay. Let's get it done, then."

The Garden District went by in a slow and beautiful blur. I was usually thinking too hard about the job I was about to do to appreciate the view.

I followed Dune into a classy lobby. Black-and-white-checked floor. Fancy lighting. A shiny-faced girl sitting at a desk in the office smiled at him, all wide-eyed and hopeful.

"Hi, Dune!" Cheery, too. Probably one of those genuinely sweet girls who had lots of friends.

"Hey." He waved and smiled back.

Jealousy roared to life, and I stepped into her line of vision.

The smile faded when she saw me. She was cute enough that I wanted to do something outrageous, like smack him on the ass or put my hand in his back pants pocket, just to make sure she was clear about where things stood.

"Her name is Jodi." He leaned over to whisper in my ear as we stepped into the elevator. "She's here on Mondays, Wednesdays, and Fridays. And she's not you, so there's nothing for you to worry about."

If Jodi had access to the camera view of the elevator, she got a good eyeful for the next thirty seconds.

Dune looked a little dazed when we exited. "Jealous Hallie is . . . I don't even have words."

"You're welcome."

He grinned and slid the key card into the slot, then took my hand and stepped into the apartment. Poe was on the couch.

"Long time no see," I said.

Poe was more than a little surprised, meaning Dune hadn't given him a heads-up, which meant Dune's loyalty was to me. I liked it.

"Hallie." He stared at our joined hands.

"That's what they call me." I didn't let go of Dune. I knew where my affections fell, and I wanted to make sure Dune knew, too. Even though jealous kissing was maybe my new favorite thing ever, and I wouldn't mind being on the receiving end of it.

Poe got right to it. "I'm sorry."

"I'm going to need a lot more than an apology."

"We have a lot to talk about," Poe agreed.

I turned to Dune. "Do you mind?"

He gave my hand a squeeze and disappeared down the hall.

Same as he was the first time I saw him, Poe was stuck somewhere between sexy and scary.

"You look like crap." I joined him on the couch.

"You look hot." British boys. Full-blown charm the second they opened their mouths. Poe and I usually had a way of understanding each other without saying a lot, but this situation was going to require multiple explanations.

"I was worried about you."

"I was worried about me, too." He lifted up his shirt.

The scar ran diagonally, obviously a slash rather than a precise cut. It was pink and raised.

"I'm assuming you didn't try to give yourself a liver transplant."

He grinned and dropped his shirt. "I assume you'd probably like to know how all this happened."

"You think?" I didn't hide the sarcasm.

"Your mom sent me to steal the Skroll. I thought it was a legit Chronos job. I didn't even think twice about it until she told me not to mention it to you or your dad."

Even though Mom hadn't worked closely with us for a while, she still assigned Chronos jobs. "That smells all kinds of shady."

"Exactly. I threw her off track and pretended I couldn't get the Skroll open."

"But you did get it open."

"Not me. Dr. Turner. I had to return it to Teague before he finished reading all the information. He tried to get it back, but your mom suspected something was up." Poe stared at his fist as he flexed it. "And then, the next day, he was gone."

"I didn't even know you knew him. How did you meet?"

"Long story. But he believed in me when no one else did."

Something told me not to push. "He told Dad how the Infinityglass gene worked before he died. We know something triggered it, but we don't know what."

"I've been trying to help Dune figure it out." He pointed

at his laptop on the kitchen table. A neat stack of index cards and a crystal skull pencil holder, with multicolor pens, sat beside it.

"So you're helping the Hourglass now?"

"No." He frowned. "I'm helping you."

"They're different from Chronos in so many ways." I leaned back on the arm of the couch. "The Hourglass keeps Dune . . . informed, at least."

"That's not the only difference. I was in Ivy Springs. I saw the way they all worked together. The kind of jobs they do. They help people."

"And?" I asked.

"It was impressive. I guess that's what it's like to work for the good guys."

"That makes Chronos the bad guys."

"Are the jobs we do there legit? Do we help the people who need it, or the ones who can afford it?"

"I don't know. But the reason you fell for Mom's bull is because we never questioned anything."

"It opened my eyes." He looked at me. "I don't want to be that guy anymore. Do you want to be that girl?"

"Do I have a choice?"

"I know you think you're invincible, Hallie, but you aren't. Every time your mom takes a chance to get what she wants, the consequences are worse. I don't want to see you on the receiving end of whatever Teague does to manipulate you next."

"I don't want to see it, either. But Dad's cut her out of Chronos now. We don't have to deal with her."

"I don't," Poe said. "You do. She's your mother."

"That's just blood. And in my book? Choice wins out over blood every time."

Dune

Hallie walked into my room without knocking. "Are you always this organized?"

"I actually am."

"Impressive."

"How did it go with Poe?" I asked.

"Fine." I could see her, trying to convince herself to believe her own lie. My hackles rose.

"Do I need to go have a talk with Poe?"

"No, no. It wasn't anything he did. Just some fair points he brought up about Chronos. And my mom."

"Do you want to talk about it?"

"No. Not yet. But Dune? Thanks."

Instead of meeting my eyes, she leaned over my desk and looked at the small corkboard Emerson had filled with pictures as a going-away present. "Ever wish you'd stayed there, in Ivy Springs?"

"Never." I sat down on the edge of the bed.

"What happened here?" The picture she was pointing to was mostly metallic silver.

"My friend Michael's room. We wrapped everything we could in aluminum foil."

"I'll have to remember that." She moved closer. "Who's he?"

I looked over her shoulder. "Nate. You'd love him. He's a dancer, too."

"And has good hair. Hold on a second." She pointed at another picture. "Speaking of hair . . . you had dreads. How long did you have dreads?"

"Pretty much always."

She turned around, her hands on her hips. "When did you cut them?"

"Right about the time I decided to come here. I didn't want to give your dad any reason to turn me down. I wanted to help you." I shrugged.

"You had to give things up. Your home, friends—and your hair—all to come to New Orleans. For me."

"Coming here wasn't mandatory. It was my choice. And don't doubt for a second that I wouldn't do the same all over again."

"The dreads were hot." She bent toward me, smoothed her fingers over my hair. "But this . . . being able to slide my hands in and keep your face where I want it? I like that better."

I met her eyes. "I might need a demonstration."

She smiled, slowly, and pulled me in for a kiss.

Chapter 15
Hallie

I wasn't done with the kissing by any means, but I couldn't stop thinking about the pictures or his life in Ivy Springs. I took the corkboard off his desk and climbed into his lap.

"Who are they?" I pointed to a group picture. "Them first."

"Kaleb and Lily," Dune said. "She can find things; he can read emotional time lines."

"That's a lot of sexy in one couple." Kaleb stood behind Lily, with his arms around her waist.

Dune laughed. "You got that right."

My jealousy tweaked a little. "And these two?"

"Emerson and Michael. Travelers. They set off electrical equipment when they touch."

"So do Amelia and Zooey. Imagine how their mom felt when they were in her womb."

I refocused on the photo. Tall, dark, and handsome held

hands with short, blond, and cute, and they both looked fierce, like anyone who tried to come between them would get taken out.

"And you never had anyone?"

"I hadn't met you yet."

I turned around to face him. "Why are you giving me puppy eyes?"

"I thought you were going to kiss me."

"Oh, keep looking at me like that and I can do better than kiss you." I put the corkboard down and slid my hands inside the short sleeves of his shirt and up, just to touch skin I hadn't before. I stopped when I saw the tattoo that completely covered his right shoulder. I pulled up the fabric and stared at the intricate lines.

"A tattoo?" The sexy surprises never stopped with this one. I wondered if there were more and made the resolution to go exploring.

"It's Samoan. Descendants of chiefs usually get the traditional *pe'a*."

"What's a *pe'a*?"

"The *pe'a* goes from the waist to the knees. *Everywhere* between the waist and the knees."

I blinked. "Do you . . . ?"

"I opted out." He grinned. "It takes ten days. If an intended chief received it and didn't cry from the pain or die from infection, he was fit to rule."

"That's . . . terrifying."

"I'll never be a chief, so the shoulder was the better option."
He looked down at it. "It stands for a lot of things. All of them
important enough for me to carry around for life."

I pushed him down on the bed. "Who are you and where did
you come from and how did I get lucky enough to be here with
you now?"

His answer was his fingertips on my face, my neck, the small
of my back. So gentle, so careful. He found sensitive spots, teased
me with his touch, and then brought every ounce of focus back to
our joined mouths.

When my explorations got a little adventurous, he rolled
me over, took my wrists in his hands, and put them over my
head. Then he adjusted our bodies so nothing but our lips were
touching.

"Dune." I pressed toward him, yearning for more. I'd have
begged for him in the middle of the Saint Louis Cathedral during
Easter mass.

"You sound winded."

"You're withholding."

"I'm delaying gratification." He lowered his body half an inch.

I was two seconds away from levitating.

"Delay this." I managed to work one leg free, and I hooked it
around the back of his knee.

His answering groan was bliss. He turned on his side and
pulled me to his chest. "We have to talk."

"No idea where you're going with this, but I can already tell you I don't like it." I started wiggling.

"Stop." He held me closer, kissing me on the forehead. "It's not bad. It's just not your usual MO. A few people from the Hourglass are coming to help us."

"A few people?" I said, stunned.

"Yes. The ones you saw in the pictures. Except for Nate. He's on a job with another friend, Ava."

'That's a lot of people." I twitched. "Why can't we handle this on our own?"

"I don't work alone, Hal. The Hourglass was always part of that for me, and you're part of it now, too, whether you like it or not."

Overwhelmed didn't touch my emotional state. "I'm not really a team player."

"I know."

"I'm not good with groups." I stood up.

So did he. "I hear you."

"I don't depend on other people. Not really." Not since Benny.

"Now you can."

Dune

"Talk to me. Where's your head?" I asked.

She started laughing. "It's just sad. I need help to handle my own mother."

"Have you ever called her out on the way she treats you?"

"What am I supposed to say? 'Hey, Mom. You suck at this. Love me more. For once, put me first. Make five minutes about me instead of always making it about you. Hear me. Damn it, just *look* at me.'"

"You could start there."

"There's no point." Hallie threw up her hands. "She'll never hear it."

"Maybe it's more important simply to say it."

"Right." Her expression closed in on itself. "If you want the Hourglass here, you're going to have to ask Dad."

"Don't change the subject."

She gave my floor a good stare-down. "Do you know how demeaning it feels to talk about how little your own parent cares for you? Especially to someone who matters?"

"Nothing you ever say should make you feel that way." I lifted her chin with my hand, saw the emotional wound in her eyes. It wasn't the kind she could heal in a second. "Especially since I care about you, too."

"You mean that."

"I do. I want you to believe it."

"You're doing a good job of proving it." She rose up on her tiptoes and pressed her lips to mine. "And you haven't even been trying."

"I hope I'm around to try later. 'Cause now I have to talk to your dad."

As we approached Hallie's house, I didn't know if I was more afraid of pissing off Paul Girard or pissing on myself.

"I'll be right there." She pointed to her dance studio. "I'll leave my phone on in case you need a lift to the hospital."

"You aren't helping."

"I wasn't trying to. I don't want you to sustain injury." She held up crossed fingers, and then she was gone.

I wished I'd added another swipe of deodorant as I walked to Girard's office and knocked on the open door. "Sir? I'd like a minute, if you have one?"

"Come in."

I handed over the crystal ball we'd stolen from the hotel.

He nodded and put it on his desk. "No problems?"

"No, sir." I didn't move.

"Is there something else?"

"Yes, sir." I didn't mean to blurt it out, but my mouth had other ideas. "I want to bring in some of my friends—colleagues—from the Hourglass."

He studied me for a second. "Can't handle this by yourself?"

"It's not that." I pulled at the collar of my shirt, and then dropped my hands, trying for confident body language. I just needed my armpits to agree. "There was a development last night. A serious one."

I explained the possessions and watched him pale.

"Is my daughter all right?" he demanded, standing up and starting for the door.

"Wait." I held up my hand. "She's fine. She's in her studio."

Now he stopped cold. "Does she know you're telling me this?"

I shook my head.

"But she's okay?"

"Yes, Mr. Girard. I swear."

"Trying to get back in my good graces?" He crossed the room to a table that held crystal tumblers and an almost empty bottle of Maker's Mark, poured a glass, and looked me over. "You broke your promise to me in the first week of your employment. The only reason you're still here is because Hallie drives a hard bargain."

"No, sir. Hallie is the priority. The protocol needs to change. I'm the only person here who can see the same things she can, besides Poe, and they aren't on speaking terms." *That you know about.*

He took a drink. "Your reserves. How many are there?"

"Four."

"I have to go out of town for a couple of days. I was content to leave Hallie in the care of my security staff, since that's the way we usually handle things, but I don't think that's going to cut it." He rubbed his upper lip. Took another drink. Paced. "I can hire all the bodyguards I want, but they don't know the players or the stakes, and there's an advantage to numbers."

"I'm not sure I understand what you mean, sir."

"Are your friends male or female?"

"Two of each."

He nodded. "We have three fully equipped guest rooms, as long as you don't mind doubling up."

I did the math and frowned. "That's six—"

"I want you and Poe here, too."

Suddenly, I was really glad he hadn't guessed the nature of the relationship between Hallie and me.

"There will still be security, and the ladies will be located very far away from the gentlemen, but if all of you can see what she can, then you can try to protect her from it. I'll be in touch with the guards while I'm gone. If things don't stay aboveboard, I'll reassess."

I knew, in this case, *reassess* meant I'd be fired, and if he found out about Hallie and me, possibly castrated.

"Yes, sir," I said.

"Take care of my daughter."

"I'll guard her with my life."

Chapter 16

Hallie

*D*une was in my dad's office. I just hoped I would hear the ambulance over the music.

Since I was alone, I decided on a quick session of warm-ups. The familiar routine usually allowed me to leave myself behind, just for a while. I tried to let my mind float, but Dune eased his way in, keeping me anchored.

Even so, I let out a shriek when I saw him at the window.

I opened the door and waved him inside. "You're not dead. That's good."

"Are there cameras in here?" he asked.

"Not in the changing room."

He grabbed my hand, dragged me in, and shut the door. Then he planted a fat one on my lips, and opened the door again.

"Not that I'm complaining, but what the hell is going on?"

I was still in the dressing room, but he was already out in the studio proper.

"The Hourglass is on the way," he said.

"He said yes." I was shocked. Dune had been in his office fifteen minutes, max.

"They're staying here."

My stomach pitched. "Okay."

"So is Poe."

I stared at him.

"And so am I."

We waited at NOLA, Emeril's restaurant on Saint Louis Street.

"Are you okay?" Dune asked.

"I'm shell-shocked."

"They were already halfway here."

I nodded. "What if Dad had said no?"

"They would've stayed in a hotel." He took my hand. "They want to help you, Hallie. It's not like they're coming down so we can all do illicit drugs and have orgies."

I snort laughed. "How did we get permission to meet them in the Quarter?"

"Your dad's setting up extra surveillance and he wanted you out of the house while he put it in," he confessed.

"You're a tech genius." I grinned, thinking about how

he'd looked on my bed. "How long will it take to reroute it?"

"I'm not going to. I promised your dad I'd take care of you, and I intend to keep it."

It was too late for lunch and too early for dinner. The place was almost empty, except for the waitstaff preparing for the evening rush. The quiet was getting to me.

Then the front door burst open.

"We're here!" A blond blur zipped across the room, followed closely by a guy with dark, shaggy hair.

"Glad to see you." The guy did the handshake-and-one-armed-hug combo with Dune before he held his hand out to me. "Hi, Hallie."

"Hi, Michael." I recognized him from the picture I'd seen in Dune's bedroom. He had the self-confidence of someone much older. "That makes you Emerson." I turned to face her.

"Hi." In person, the perky cuteness I'd seen in the photo was tempered with something. Sorrow in her eyes, but strength, too. "We're all so glad to meet you."

Now Dune hugged a guy with a few piercings and visible tattoos.

"Kaleb," the guy said, turning to me. The picture hadn't done him justice. "Thanks for having us."

"According to Dune, you were all going to visit, anyway."

Kaleb grinned. "That's the way we do."

"I'm Lily." She gave me a beautiful and genuine smile. Kaleb tucked his arm around her. They were breathtaking.

Ten to one they did it with the lights on.

"Welcome to New Orleans," I said a little too brightly. "Let's get some hospitality going."

We took a seat and ordered, the lights above the table dimming slightly when Michael and Emerson bumped hands. Same as with Amelia and Zooey, it calmed after a few seconds. Everyone talked a hundred miles an hour, catching up while we waited. Except for me, since I had nothing to catch up on. I held Dune's hand under the table and observed.

Lily and Emerson both made attempts to pull me into the conversation, but they were gentle attempts. Kaleb rivaled paid entertainment, engaging everyone, but Michael was quiet. Enough to make me feel comfortable, like I wasn't the only person at the table who wasn't a talker.

Dune leaned close to whisper in my ear. "They like you. I can tell."

"I like them, too," I whispered back. "But I have no idea what to say."

"You'll figure it out. Or they'll figure it out for you."

He was right. They were so comfortable with one another that it extended to me, instead of excluding me. I understood what Poe meant now. They were impressive as a team. They were impressive humans.

After dinner, which I didn't eat, Dune, Lily, Kaleb, and I headed toward Bourbon. Em and Michael set out to find a Laissez Les Bons Temps Rouler baby onesie.

"Planning ahead?" I asked Dune as they walked away.

"Em's about to be an aunt."

"I'm guessing Michael will eventually be the uncle?" I wondered if the tiny article of clothing would be recycled to their child one day.

"Probably."

Lily touched my arm. "What should we know about the Quarter? Isn't it dangerous at night?"

"It can be, but there's some serious bulk in this group," I said. "I mean, not me and you, obviously, but we have the Rock and the Hulk as personal bodyguards."

"I do not turn green." Kaleb shook his head. "Ever."

"Just when any guy looks at Lily for longer than five seconds," Dune said. "Which is a lot."

I sensed I'd be doing some jealous kissing later.

"Okay," Kaleb admitted. "I've totally considered going 'Hulk smash!' More than once."

Dune nodded as he took my hand. "I know the feeling, man."

Lily winked at me, and I decided to do some thank-you kissing now.

"Head that way. We'll be right behind you." I pointed Lily and Kaleb toward Saints & Sinners. Then I pushed Dune into an alley.

"What are you—"

I steered him where I wanted him to go, until his back was against a brick wall. "I wish we still had the room at the Bourbon Orleans."

189

"I'm glad, but I'm confused. Where is this coming from?"

"Your friends are sweet to me." I tucked two fingers in his waistband. "You're sweet to me. You make me feel like a completely normal girl."

"If making you feel normal gets this kind of response, remind me to do it more often."

I slid my hands up his stomach to his chest, and then around his neck. His hands went down, over my waist and hips and stopping on my backside. I was beyond pleased when a low groan sounded in his throat.

"We are in an alley." His mouth was on my cheek, my neck, and going lower. "In the very, very public French Quarter."

"That doesn't seem to be stopping you." I leaned my head back to give him easy access.

"I can't. I want to touch you all the time." Lifting me up, he turned the tables and put my back against the wall. "I want to be with you all the time. Talk to you all the time."

"Talking is good. Not that I'm interested in conversation right now." I wrapped my legs around his waist, and his hands moved to the backs of my thighs. His weight against me was mind-blowing. "Did I mention how much I wished we still had a room? I'm hanging on you like a tick."

"I'm holding you like a life vest."

"We're not good at sexy imagery."

He started laughing. "Do you want me to put you down?"

"No. I want to stay in this exact moment. Well, maybe where

we'd end up in thirty minutes if this progressed the way I wanted, but we have work to do, and I just sent your friends to a celebrity bar, and I think I see a hobo coming, so we better go."

One more kiss, and then I slid down his body slowly. I laughed when his eyes rolled back in his head. After I was sure we were both presentable and tucked in, I took his hand and stepped out of the alley.

Mardi Gras had come to New Orleans. On a Saturday.

Three months early.

Twenty years too late.

Dune

"Dune, wait." Hallie stopped at the alley entryway. "Something isn't right."

The number of people on Bourbon Street had tripled. There were way more plastic beads and masks with feathers than usual for this time of year. Music blared, the crowds were raucous, and alcohol permeated.

Utter chaos.

Hallie took my hand and pulled me in the direction she'd indicated to Kaleb and Lily. We found them on the sidewalk, looking confused.

"It isn't there." Kaleb's voice barely carried over the noise of the revelers on the sidewalk as he pointed to where Saints &

Sinners used to be. "We saw the sign, and then we didn't."

I turned to Hallie and tried to pitch my voice over the heavy sound around us. "Do you recognize anything?"

She wrinkled her nose as she scanned the crowd. "Beer and sweat with a top note of vomit is how it usually smells here, but I'm guessing from the costumes, this is Mardi Gras. Parades on Bourbon were rerouted in the seventies. Oh, look. Love beads and Birkenstocks."

"Great," I replied. "The sixties. Booze and free love. Way to keep it classy, space time continuum."

Kaleb took stock of the throng of people around us. "Look around. It's not just the sixties."

"I don't see any eighties bangs. I don't think it goes beyond the seventies, just back in time. And . . . the buildings have changed. Kaleb." Lily grabbed his arm. "This is a rip world."

My blood turned to stone. "It's sucked us in."

"How do we get out?" Hallie's voice was frantic as she focused on the people around us. Not people, rips.

They stopped to stare at Hallie.

And then they started toward her, moving as one.

Chapter 17
Hallie

I could feel them coming.

"You can see them?" I asked Dune, squeezing his hand.

"I can."

"They know what I am." Panic made my heart race as my joints went loose. "They know, and they want me."

Dune kept his voice as low as he could in the middle of the crowd, speaking into my ear. "I won't leave you, Hal, I swear."

My shirt was soaked with sweat. "Get me away from them."

Dune didn't wait for me to finish. He jerked me toward the alley we'd just left, running hard, pulling on my hand. Lily and Kaleb followed.

We were close, approaching the corner of the alley, almost there. So very close.

But the rips were closer.

Images rushed around me like water swirling down a drain. It happened so much faster than before, maybe because we were trapped in the rips' world, instead of them being trapped in ours.

My body became a revolving door for rips. The blood in my veins pumped double time, triple time, as my cells regenerated and tried to give me enough energy to handle what was coming.

The mask is more than a Mardi Gras favor; it's my chance to find Jean Claude, to make him mine.

I approach the entryway where he's agreed to meet me, finally, and his arm reaches out to sweep me into the darkness. He says not a word, but his hands ravage my body. They grip my waist, my hips, linger on the curve of my breasts above the corset. Air kisses my skin as he pulls down my sleeves and his lips find my shoulder.

"Take off the mask," I command. "I've waited so long for you."

Heat rolls off his body, and tension keeps his muscles tight. "Here, in the dark?" he asks, tracing the neckline of my gown. "Instead of a bed?"

"Now." He reaches for my mask, mindful of the feathers. He knows I must go back to my husband tonight. His mouth claims mine before I can tell him to mind the lipstick, and I decide I don't care.

New world, new players.

"I don't want to show you anything," the girl yells back at me. I laugh and drop the beads for her, anyway.

I feel generous here. New Orleans is good to me. The beer is cold, and no one ever asks for my name. No one cares. About anything. Not if I drink, not if I squat, not if I steal. At the right parties, they don't even care if I crawl into bed with them. If I get that far, they don't care what I do next.

I stick my hand in my pocket. Wince when I catch a hangnail. Two rings, a wallet, cash. A set of car keys, a checkbook, and my favorite, a tiny knife with a pearl handle. A knife that sliced my cheek open before dinnertime, but belonged to me by sunset.

I can steal bigger things with a knife. I can hurt someone with a knife.

Will anyone care about that?

The possession let up long enough for me to reach out for Dune. I could feel him, hear him, but the next round slammed into me, swallowing me whole.

"Did you hear?" Carolina is aflutter, her fan flipping her ringlets at a furious pace. "The scandal is international. She buried bodies beneath the floorboards."

Elizabeth has more to share. "There were experiments in the attic. She'd peeled back skin and let people—"

"Stop." I speak too loudly for a lady, but my stomach is churning. "This isn't a thing to sensationalize. These were human beings. People, with souls."

"But they were just slaves."

I stare at Carolina, wondering how her heart can be so full of darkness. How we could've been raised in the same household. How she can

have such disregard for human life. "You should be ashamed of yourself.
I'm ashamed to call you sister."

My request doesn't stop her. "Men and women were chained to the
wall, body parts scattered all around in piles and in buckets. . . ."

I cover my mouth with my handkerchief, my stomach churning at
the thought of so much human pain, and the knowledge that my own
flesh and blood relished it.

No more ugliness or horror. I pushed the memory away,
but they wouldn't let me go. Instead they just came faster and
faster. . . .

Dune

I sat on the ground, her head in my lap. The rips shuffled her
cells like they were a card deck, forming them into their own
images.

Kaleb's focus shifted from the rips on the street to Hallie on
the ground. "What the hell is going on?"

"Rips. Funneling through her, controlling her."

"Her face . . ." Lily reached out to put her hand on Hallie's
arm, hovering just above it. Tears filled her eyes. "Kaleb and I
might know a way out, but I'm scared of what could happen to
Hallie if the rip world dissolves while she's possessed."

"So am I." I pushed Hallie's hair out of her face, one that no
longer belonged to her. The faces of those possessing her moved

so fast her own features were a blur. She was underneath. She needed me.

Kaleb's eyes were guarded. "We've got to stop this."

"I don't know how. She's broken free from it on her own before. I never made her do it."

"Dune?" Lily's voice broke through my thoughts. "You need to see this."

The alley was still dark, but the sound of the party on the street echoed off the walls. The streetlights illuminated what had put so much fear in Lily's voice.

The rips that had noticed us on Bourbon, at least thirty of them, were lined up across the entrance of the alley. Every single one stared at Hallie.

"Hallie. Come back." Please.

As if she heard me, the transmutations slowed enough for me to distinguish some features.

A middle-aged woman with too much lipstick, most of it smeared.

A younger guy with a gash on his left cheek.

A girl Hallie's age, her hair in ringlets and tears in her eyes.

The same faces were reflected in the rips' lining the alley.

And then I caught a brief glimpse of Hallie, and she whispered my name. "Dune."

"I'm here." I grabbed her hands. "Open your eyes."

Hallie groaned a little and her eyelids fluttered. When she gritted her teeth and squeezed my hands, I realized what she was doing.

"She's trying to control the rip. She's pulling it in."

In the street where the Mardi Gras parade raged on, a bright light flashed and narrowed. The rips began to fade around the edges. A premonition pushed into my brain.

Suddenly, the rip world began folding in on itself. Inches faded at a time, and then inches became feet. The rips lining the alley disappeared all at once, and then everything was gone except for Hallie. There were a few seconds of peace, and I thought it was over.

I was wrong.

Voices roared. A gravitational pull fought against our hands, tugging at Hallie, snatching at her hair. The force of it moved her across the ground, toward the light, and Lily and Kaleb grabbed her arms.

They were fighting for her as hard as I was, but she had to fight for herself.

"Don't leave me, Hallie." I had to yell over the chaos.

Her eyes flew open and locked on mine.

"I'm not ready to lose you!" The whirling air around us snatched my words as they came out of my mouth. But Hallie heard me.

"I'm not ready to go." She sat up. Her whole body tensed as a scream that sounded like a thousand voices ripped its way out of her. Power surged through the alley, and the roaring ceased.

In one short second, the darkness swallowed the light, leaving us in complete silence.

Chapter 18
Hallie

I slept for five hours.

When I woke up, Dune was in my bed with me, typing one hand. The other was on my hip. "Dune?"

"Hey." After a couple more key clicks, he put the computer down and kissed my forehead. "What can I get for you? What do you need?"

"You." I grabbed him and held on tightly. It took less than a second for him to hold on harder.

"You slept for a long time." He tucked my hair behind my ears. "I think you took about thirty thousand breaths."

Because he watched every single one.

"Where are the houseguests?" I asked.

"Kaleb and Lily went to find Michael and Em so I could bring you straight home. They're all back. Probably asleep."

"I don't remember what happened."

"It was a rip world. The whole thing took us over. Not only did you stop your possessions, you got us out, too."

"How?" I asked.

"I hoped you'd remember. Poe saved Em and Michael from a rip world once, but it was a totally different situation." His lips touched mine, and he smiled with his eyes. "You saved our lives."

I climbed on top of him and dropped my forehead to his shoulder. Images of some of the people who'd possessed me flickered in my subconscious, but I didn't want to recall any of it.

"You cried in your sleep. I couldn't decide whether or not to wake you up."

"Bad dreams. The night I was possessed in the ballroom, there were happy moments. Everything I saw in that alley tonight was terrible, depraved in some way. I don't want the memories, but I have them."

"Do you want to talk about it?"

"Not now." Maybe never.

"Whatever you need, I'm here."

"You're here." I sat up straight. "In my bed. My dad is going to kill you!"

"No, he's not. Carl is heading up security tonight, and after I told him what happened, he didn't want you left alone any more than I did. I put the security feed on a loop, just for tonight. We're safe."

"Look at you, taking care of me." I wanted to touch his

skin, not the cotton of his T-shirt. I pulled it over his head and was almost disappointed when I didn't see more tattoos than the one on his shoulder. Then I ran my hands over his chest, and all disappointment left the building. Smooth skin. Defined muscles.

Floaty hearts. Falling. I let my fingertips absorb the warmth of him and hoped it would smother the nightmares.

"Tell me about your tattoo. You said you wanted to keep these memories for life."

He explained the different parts as I traced over them. "The swirls stand for past, present, and future."

"Is that a turtle?" I would've expected a sea animal to look hokey, but it didn't on him.

He gave me his crinkle smile, like he knew what I was thinking. "They have remarkable migratory patterns. They always return home."

I leaned over to place a kiss in the center of the turtle's shell. "And the word *aiga*?"

"It means 'family.' The ten stars represent everyone I've lost, and the moon is for my father."

I hoped he didn't have to add any more stars. My sigh caught on a sob, but I stopped myself before it broke.

"Hey." He lifted my chin with one finger. "Like I said tonight, I'm not going to lose you."

"You saved me in that alley; you didn't leave. You or your friends." I couldn't imagine what I would do if Dune weren't part of my life. "You stayed, and gave me a reason to hold on."

As if he heard the words I couldn't utter, he said, "I'm not going anywhere. Not without you."

I moved to the skin over his heart, placed a kiss there. "I don't want that, either. Not ever."

"Hallie." He spoke my name in a whisper.

He was watching me. Raw, unmasked. All that control conquered. Finally.

"Dune," I whispered back.

His fingers dug into my hips, holding me back, but his expression didn't change. "A lot of terrible things went down tonight."

"Yes, they did. Good reason to claim a stake on life, don't you think?"

"All I can think about is trying to stop this."

"Are you saying you don't want to kiss me?" I traced the outline of his bottom lip, staring at his mouth. "Are you really going to tell me no?"

"Yes, I want to kiss you. I'm not insane. And who could possibly tell you no?"

I had time to smile before his kisses burned down the column of my throat, across my collarbone. He took my face in his hands, leaned back, and brought my mouth down to his.

I let myself sink into the kiss, into him.

When he rolled me over and covered my body with his own, I lost my breath.

Dune thought he was so quiet, sneaking out of bed. When a 220-pound weight lifted, a girl noticed.

I'd slept enough, but I stayed quiet, letting him think I was still out cold. I had a lot to think about, and he'd spent a good part of the past hour making sure I hadn't thought at all.

When he shut the door behind him, I opened my eyes. His laptop was open on my desk. I didn't hesitate.

I clicked on the external hard drive that held all the Infinityglass info. I didn't look at anything else on his computer. I didn't want to invade his privacy. I just wanted a quick look at the things that pertained to me that I hadn't seen yet. No one could fault that.

Especially if I didn't get caught.

There were carefully labeled folders organized by year, and one with the words *time-related objects* underneath. I found other folders with lists of links, articles scanned from old newspapers, and thumbnails of pictures, one of which showed an hourglass in a frame made out of human bones. It had been stolen from a museum.

By me.

Others were things I'd never seen or heard of, and while some of them were truly scary, others seemed downright ridiculous. I kept skimming until I found a folder with my initials on it, and then I was overcome by that undeniable feeling of anxiety that arrives when you're seeing something you shouldn't.

That didn't stop me from clicking.

Three other names occupied my desktop file, each with folders of their own.

Two females, one male.

Very little information was provided. One of the girls helped on an archeological dig that took place around the time Tut's tomb was discovered, in the golden age of archeology. The other worked on a farm, possibly in the United Kingdom, and listed no dates.

The guy's folder had nothing but a name and a GPS location.

I scanned the rest of the information.

Scientific terms, mathematical equations—gibberish to me. I closed out the hard drive and saw a minimized document I'd missed before. It didn't even have a title, so it must have been what Dune was typing when I woke up.

There were notes about activation, with more questions than answers, and paragraphs written in another language: what looked like Arabic or Egyptian. There were also photographs of hieroglyphs.

Attempted translations were directly below the pictures, and one phrase in bold jumped off the page.

I read it. Twice.

And went to find Dune.

Dune

I'd tried to be quiet getting out of bed. Hallie needed rest, but there was no way I was sleeping after tonight.

I went down to grab a drink and found Poe in the kitchen.

"Popsicles again?" I asked.

"Picked them up on the way over, after you called." He shut the freezer door and met my eyes. "Is Hallie okay?"

"She's asleep. She got us out, Poe. We'd still be in that alley without her." I stepped around him to the fridge, took out a bottle of water. "Something clicked for me tonight. Have you seen the section of the Skroll about the Infinityglass and the transfer of abilities?"

Poe crossed his arms over his chest. "Yeah, but I don't know how it works. Do you?"

"I don't." Worry was all I knew. "Only that it results in death."

He met my eyes. "Not Hallie's. It can't. I don't think something as powerful as the Infinityglass is a one-time-use type of weapon."

I rubbed the back of my neck, and then growled in frustration. "I want this to be resolved, and I want a mathematical, scientific formula that makes sense from beginning to end. Not mythology. Not fairy dust. Real answers that I can work with."

"I hate to bring you down even more, but I've not made any progress. I can't find out what activated Hallie's Infinityglass ability. I've read and reread the Skroll. I've made lists of every-thing we've stolen in the past few months and researched every piece. I thought it could have been this clock, but it's not. You said something clicked for you. What was it?"

"The Infinityglass is supposed to have ultimate power over the space time continuum, but since everything is screwed up, I don't think that's the case anymore. I've been translating the foreign language docs on the Skroll bit by bit, and one finished up tonight."

"And?"

"I think the space time continuum is using Infinityglass Hallie as a power source, or at least the rips are. And I think it could deplete her. There's something about the rips and the way they keep trying to pull her in—"

I heard a noise and held up one finger.

Ten seconds later, Hallie walked into the kitchen.

Messy hair, red lips, and loose limbs. She swiped the water bottle out of my hand, opened it, and took a long drink. In that moment, all I could think about was dragging her back to her room and shutting out the world. That thought disappeared real quick when she lowered the bottle.

"When were you going to tell me there's a death sentence on my head?"

Neither Poe or I answered. Or moved.

"I just spent some quality time with your computer," she said, handing the water back to me. "I want to know what's going on. Put it in layman's terms, professors."

"We don't know anything definite," Poe started, but she held up one hand.

"How about you go back to what you stopped discussing right before I walked in here, about science and magic? Depletion?" She pointed to her ears. "Super-duper hearing these days, remember?"

Poe moved to the table and sat down, but said nothing.

Hallie looked back and forth between us. "The man who passes the sentence should swing the sword. So one of you tell me what you know."

I looked at Poe. I was the one with the theory, and I hadn't even gotten a chance to explain it to him. I'd be swinging this sword by myself. I turned my attention to Hallie. "You saw my notes."

"I sure did."

"There's a theory that the Infinityglass can be used to transfer abilities from one person with the time gene to another. Everything that's translated recently . . . suggests it involves death. I don't know whose, but I'm assuming it's not yours."

Her face paled. "Keep going."

"What I was just getting ready to explain to Poe is that the transmutation ability means your cells regenerate constantly, faster than normal, which is what allows you to change your appearance."

"He knows all that. So do I. Why are you teaching Hallie 101?"

"There's a progression," I said gently. "Listen, okay?"

Pressing her lips together, she pulled out the chair beside Poe's and sat.

"Once the Infinityglass part of you became activated, your transmutation ability sped up and got stronger," I continued. "Everything about you got stronger, right? Super-human hearing, vision, energy."

She nodded.

"The rips are using you as a power source. As long as they can possess you, they can live. They aren't going to give you up without a fight."

She stared down at her hands. "What happens if I lose?"

My throat felt like I'd swallowed a bucket of sawdust. "I don't know, but we'll find answers. Between what we're learning every day, and the number of people trying to help, and the wealth of information we already have . . . we'll find answers."

"How can I avoid them? They find me. If they want to take me over . . ."

Poe covered one of her hands with his briefly and then stood. "Dune's right, Hallie. We're going to get answers. I *will* figure out what got you in this position, and then I'll learn how to reverse it."

He left the kitchen, and Hallie and I stared at each other through silence.

"Are you okay?" I asked.

"No. It's just a matter of time before it happens again. What if I don't get out next time?"

I pulled her into my arms, rested my chin on top of her head. "You will."

I wanted to believe it, but things were happening too fast. The truths about the Infinityglass came slowly at first, but now the terrible possibilities were tumbling toward us in a rush.

At what I feared was the end of the story.

Chapter 19

Hallie

*D*une sat at my desk, scrolling and clicking.

We'd sent the Hourglass contingent out to sightsee. I'd spent the day staring at my TV and tried to lose myself in a *Supernatural* marathon, but I was too stressed out to enjoy the eye candy. Finally, I clicked the remote and stood.

"Off." I closed the lid of his laptop, barely missing his fingers, and sending empty Jolly Rancher candy wrappers skittering to the floor. "All you've done is stare at that damn computer all day."

He raised a brow. "Just trying to find answers."

I dropped onto the bed. "Sit with me."

He didn't touch me when he did. I took it metaphorically.

"We aren't going to do this, Dune." I gestured to the empty space. "You're removing yourself from the situation, and removing yourself from me."

"This isn't about distance. It's about giving you room to breathe. Giving me time to research."

"I want us in the same airspace right now, okay? I need it."

Dune's arms were around me in a second. "I need it, too."

Relief eased my tension before his mouth on mine ratcheted it up again—gentle, insistent—not enough.

I wrapped my arms around his waist and pressed my body to his. Closing my eyes, I teased his mouth open to deepen the kiss. He tasted like candy. "Forgiven."

"I'm still sorry. I didn't think circling the same thing over and over again in conversation would be good for us, and I didn't have any new answers."

"I understand, but I don't want to lose time with you now. What if I can't get it back later?"

His thumb smoothed over my forehead and down my temple. "We're going to figure out how to stop the rips from taking over."

This was the capable Dune, the one everyone looked to for ideas and support. Totally solid, completely dependable. He thought he was nothing more than the strength behind the scenes. "As much as I've tried to avoid being trapped in one place my whole life, now I don't want to move from this spot. I keep thinking, *Can they find me here? Am I safe here?*"

"You're as safe as I can make you."

"I know." Even though I hadn't shed a tear, I felt like I'd been crying for days. Raw, achy, and emotionally spent.

"I want to make you happy," he murmured into my hair. "Tell me how."

I whispered in his ear.

Dune pulled away so he could look into my eyes.

"I could disappear," I said. "Not exist, except as a full-time playground for dead people. I know the timing sucks, but right now is all we have."

"No, it's not, Hal. I'll make sure of it."

"You'll try. But you can't guarantee it, and I don't want to lose one more second. Do you?"

Instead of answering, he shut the bedroom door.

He hadn't fallen asleep until dawn, and even then he'd only slept in snatches. This time, I was the one who watched him take every breath. When my phone rang, I picked it up to silence it, figuring it was Dad checking in.

My heart stopped cold when I saw the name on the caller ID.

I shook Dune awake and answered.

"Hello, Mother."

She sounded cool and well rested. Wherever she'd been for the past few weeks, the living hadn't been hard.

"Where have you been?" I asked, keeping my tone as bored as I could manage. "We thought you were dead."

"Don't you mean *hoped*?"

"What do you think?"

Dune sat up beside me. The word *backup* had never meant so much. My mother's lack of response gave me a petty amount of pleasure. Today, I'd take pleasure wherever I could get it.

"Why are you calling?" I leaned back into Dune's chest. "I know you want something. You always do."

"That's no way to talk to your mother, Little Miss."

It was her childhood nickname for me, a passive-aggressive insult. Her specialty. "Whatever."

"I'm your mother. That's why I'm calling." She took a deep sigh for dramatic effect. "I want to help you. I want to lift the burden of the Infinityglass from you. I can make that happen. I can help."

I tensed, saying nothing. Waiting for the bomb to drop.

"I'm in New Orleans, and I need to see you."

"Could she be telling the truth?" Dune asked. "What if she does have a way to help?"

"Everyone should try something new once in a while. Maybe truth is her latest hobby."

Dune had insisted on neutral ground, and Audubon Park fit the bill. We took Dad's town car down Saint Charles. It dropped us off across from Tulane's Gibson Hall.

We didn't go in too deep, staying far away from the Fly, the side of the park next to the river. Even so, I could still smell the Mississippi. I knew Dune could, too. A keen edge of panic sneaked out from underneath his mask of cool every time the wind blew.

"Are you okay?" I asked, "with the water?"

"You're beautiful."

"Subject changer." I turned to face him. We hadn't recapped the events of the night before, but I couldn't stop thinking about his skin, his mouth, his hands.

"I am not. I just wanted to say what was on my mind." He pulled me down to sit beside him on a bench.

"I hope you're having the same thought I am," I said.

"Which is?"

"More."

He caught the back of my head in his hand and brought me in for a kiss. "Don't give up yet."

I nodded, and then a shadow blocked the sun. The afterglow disappeared in a flash.

"Hello, Mother."

"Hallie." She looked down her nose at Dune. "Who is this?"

"We've never officially met." He stood to shake her hand, which she did, with disdain. It didn't faze him. "I'm Dune Ta'ala."

He put his arm around me when he sat back down, keeping his body forward, as close in front of me as he could be. His eyes had gone from sweet to wary, and the scar through his eyebrow became menacing instead of intriguing.

It was the first time I'd seen him use his physicality to intimi-date, like a peacock fluffing up his plumes. It was ridiculously hot, and from the visible tension in my mother's body, it worked.

"Does your father know about this?" Mother slid her sunglasses off and put them in her purse.

"Yes," I answered, keeping my eyes on Dune.

"And what does he think about it?"

I shrugged. Let her wonder. If she'd been on the run, it had been somewhere that provided French manicures and root touchups. "You look good, but you always do. I see you've been shopping for jewelry, too. Why didn't you call me? We could've made a day of it."

She brushed her fingers just above the long, antique pendant that lay against her turtleneck sweater. "You're almost eighteen, yet you show no signs of maturity."

"You're way past forty. Neither do you."

"Nothing ever changes." She sat down on the bench across from ours.

"No, it doesn't. Probably never will. Why are you here?"

"To help my daughter."

"Please. There are a million ulterior motives in everything you do." I rubbed my temples. Oh, how this woman exhausted me.

"I'm here because of who you are." She paused for effect. "What you are. How you got that way. Wouldn't you like to know?"

"I don't need you for answers. I don't need you for anything." Her expression would have frozen a hot spring solid. In July. After a moment, all the chill melted away, and she smiled.

"Really?"

Cold dread swirled in the pit of my stomach. I knew that

smile. She had something on me, something big. She didn't seem eager to make me work for the information, which meant she could barely contain it.

That was scarier than a hundred rips coming for me at once.

"I've been with Chronos for years, ever since my own parents worked for them," she said. "I've seen raw talent that you can't even fathom." The smile faded and was replaced by calculation. "I was a scientist before I was a mother, so I had time to think about the kind of child I wanted. One just like me."

An uneasy fear crept up my spine.

"I wanted to make sure I did everything perfectly," she said, "so there was research. So much tedious research. I needed to verify the genetic sequence, so I located specimens."

"Specimens?"

Her smile made a brief reappearance. "Once everything was confirmed and reconfirmed, I began experimenting. Of course, mistakes were made."

Adrenaline numbed my face and clutched at my vocal cords. She couldn't mean what I thought she meant.

"No one gets everything right the first time. Experiments can create monsters."

"What kind of monsters?"

"The versions of you that I didn't get right the first time."

My mouth went dry. "You made multiple versions of me. Are they still out there?"

"I don't allow mistakes."

I stared at her, hoping for a shred of humanity. Searching for anything that wasn't cold and self-serving. I didn't find any of it.

"I count as a success, then?" I asked.

"You're as close as I could get."

"Did you ever love me?" I asked. God, it hurt, because I knew the answer. "Or was I just a means to an end?"

"People define *love* in their own ways," Mother said. "Some people say love is about duty. Or loyalty. You owe me your very life. The way our relationship has progressed is completely your choice."

"No, you made all my choices for me." Either through manipulation or emotional blackmail.

"Have you considered I have motives?"

The pull of the power she had over me was the only thing keeping me in my seat. I decided then and there, no matter how many hours or minutes I had left on earth, that she wasn't going to dictate one more second.

"Your motives are the least of it. I don't know one true thing about you, and I don't want to."

Dune

"You're wrong about that," Teague said to Hallie. "I think there's plenty you want to know about me. About you."

Seconds ago, sadness had hung off Hallie's frame like an empty husk. Now it disappeared and was replaced by determination.

"No, there isn't." Hallie squeezed my hand. "I'm done talking. As of *right now*."

She leaned back in her seat and imitated zipping her lips and throwing away the key. It was fiendishly immature, and just the right choice to piss Teague off.

Teague stood and turned her back on Hallie.

I had tried to check out emotionally and play the part of the cool observer, but right now I wanted to get ugly. Anger would've satisfied me on a primal level, but I chose a more balanced playing field. My weapon would be intelligence rather than emotion. I spoke up. "Tell me your motives."

When Teague turned around, I realized how much she and her daughter resembled each other. Remarkably so. I knew how beautiful Hallie would be twenty years from now. My job was to figure out how to get her there.

"I don't think so. You aren't part of this," Teague demurred. "I know your weaknesses, Dune. I know you can smell the water from here, and that it calls to you. I even know what it says."

I felt Hallie tense beside me, but thankfully she was stubborn enough to stay silent. I stood and stepped forward, completely disrespecting Teague's personal space. "I don't need a translator. Tell me, Teague, what is your goal? Power? Or is it just the idea of conquering time?"

"I don't need to share my intentions with you." Teague looked from me to Hallie. "I'm here to talk to my daughter."

"She doesn't want to talk to you. I'm the only reason she's still sitting here, so if there's something you want her to know, I'm the messenger."

Teague's eyes were a deeper hazel, but she and her daughter shared the same slender build and tall frame. Their dark hair shone like silk in the sunlight, and they had perfect bee-stung lips. But where Hallie's face was still soft, Teague's was nothing but hard angles. Less in her appearance, more in her countenance. Other than that, they were alike.

Exactly alike.

The truth sneaked in and blindsided me. I took a step back, staring at Teague. "Do you have the transmutation gene?"

Teague offered a bemused smile in response. "You and Hallie haven't discussed my ability?"

"She told me you're a human clock. You always know what time it is, down to the second without looking. Half metronome, half party trick." Hallie had also told me Teague didn't use it very much. "If you were around someone like that every day, it would get old pretty fast. It might be amusing to a child, but eventually the novelty would wear off. They'd stop asking for demonstrations. You could stop faking it."

The deep lines around her mouth told me I was on the right track.

"Instead of digging up specimens with the Infinityglass gene," I asked, "why didn't you just use your own?"

"Use my own? That's a ridiculous assumption." Teague crossed her arms over her chest. "I—"

"You couldn't take the chance that having a child naturally would create someone like you. You had to make sure the specific gene was isolated. You needed exact proof."

She leaned down to pick up her purse. "When my *daughter* is ready to talk to me, let me know."

I stepped in front of her. "How long did it take before you considered cloning?"

"Cloning?" Hallie stood, too, giving up her vow of silence.

I got out of the way and let Hallie take over.

"Is he right?"

"Not cloning. You're genetically engineered." Teague sounded bored. "It's not a quick explanation."

Hallie took a step back. "You're an Infinityglass, too."

"I'm not." Teague tilted her chin defiantly.

"She's telling the truth," I confirmed, staring Teague down. "Because she never activated, either because she didn't want to or she didn't know how. Or both."

Hallie's eyes burned with the truth. "How much of Dad's 'protection' was really you? Did you feed his paranoia to make it easier to keep me under your thumb? How much did he know?"

Teague didn't answer. She wasn't even looking at us. She was staring at a rip.

It spread across the park like an extended movie screen, the edges undulating in the breeze.

Except the air around us was still.

It expanded into a rip world bustling with industry. Buildings under construction. Workmen busy at their tasks. Shiny metal signs hung everywhere, displaying the words WORLD COTTON CENTENNIAL, 1884.

"It's the world's fair," Teague murmured.

"It's a rip world. Your first one?" Hallie asked. Her mom didn't acknowledge the question. "They get better. See the people in the present disappearing? It's because the past takes over."

Teague watched as the rip expanded again, and another building came into view. Electric lights hung everywhere, the name *Edison* prominent on all the accompanying equipment.

My chest felt like a semi had parked on it. Hallie and I'd talked about the next rip she'd encounter, and what the last one had done to her. What would this one do?

Hallie stood, her back to the rip. "You know how I feel about Jackson Square after what happened. I won't go there on a good day. There's no way in hell I'd go past the place where Benny bled to death now."

Teague's head jerked up and she focused on Hallie's face. "Why?"

"The rips come from the past, and they possess me. I troll around in their memories, and they live inside my skin. That's what being the Infinityglass means. Thank you so very much."

The rip world grew wider, taking over another section of land. A building made of glass appeared in the distance.

Hallie's focus shifted to something behind us, her eyes following it in a circle. Horses on a track. "You can blame yourself for this, Mother."

"I didn't start it," Teague said. "Jack Landers is the one who broke the rules."

"You perpetuated it. You threw in with him," Hallie argued. "You let him look for the Infinityglass, and the whole time you knew it was me."

"I kept that information from him," Teague argued back.

The rip grew wider, going around us instead of flowing over us. I put my hand on the small of Hallie's back. I needed to get her out.

"I tried to protect you, Hallie." Teague's voice trembled.

"Really?" Hallie laughed without mirth. "Don't pretend like you have feelings for me. You've never cared for me the way a mother should care for her own child, because you didn't give birth to me; you bred me."

"I created you."

The smell of manure blended with the sounds of livestock, all of it too close.

"Hal, we've gotta go. It's growing too fast to—"

The rip world moved like lightning, swallowing Hallie, and then Teague.

I did the only thing I could.

I followed.

Chapter 20
Hallie

*S*uddenly, I was staring up at a bright blue sky rather than the gray one that had been there ten seconds ago.

A crowd of rips gathered, staring at me, just like ones we'd encountered in the alley in the French Quarter.

Two seconds later, my mother appeared.

I took off running, keeping to the Saint Charles side of the park, dodging in and out of crowds. It might be impossible to outrun a rip, but I was sure as hell going to try.

"Hallie, stop!"

I paused to look over my shoulder. My mother. The woman could move in heels, I'd give her that. "Enjoying the early nineteenth century? Because there's a good chance it's about to enjoy me."

I took off again, but I'd chosen the wrong direction. The first rip caught me just outside the international exhibition.

The boy was Chinese. He sat beside a merchant, presumably his father, as they took items out of wooden shipping crates and cataloged them. He'd been crying.

"*But I don't understand why anyone would treat a human this way.*"

He spoke a language that wasn't my own, yet was. I understood it, and the source of the pain in his chest.

"*There are slaves in China.*" *Father speaks with a discordant note, not to admonish me, but to teach me.* "*The number is small, and the practice is waning, but almost every culture has a race that they treat as half man, half thing.*"

"*I will never treat a human with anything resembling this contempt.*" *I make the vow to myself and to my family's honor.*

"*I know, son of mine. This is why I brought you here, to America. To see the different ways people live, and so you can choose your own path. Kindness is always the answer. Turn your inner concerns outward, and live for others rather than yourself.*"

My father grins and holds up a tiny golden Buddha. "*It doesn't hurt if you sell them a few things along the way.*"

When I opened my eyes, I was on the ground, on my back.

My mother had seen the possession, watched it change my body, and she was afraid. "Your face . . ."

I didn't have time to enjoy her fear. I was too busy anticipating an onslaught. What I saw when I looked around rocked me to the core.

The rips were watching us. Not me, *us*. Me and my mother.

Some held back, and others surged forward to stare. Even though they drifted closer to me than her, they still hovered, unable to keep their eyes in one place. Unable to make a decision.

"Do you see that?" I asked her softly. "They can't decide if they want to pick me or you. You might not be activated, but you're still an Infinityglass."

"Maybe. But you're the powerful one." She said the words loudly, like she wanted to make sure they could hear. And then she pointed. "She's the powerful one."

The rips knew their best option, and now they were advancing. I felt the pull, but it wasn't as strong as usual. I guessed I had something to thank my mother for after all, even if it was only a momentary distraction.

I moved closer to her. The rips followed me, and once again split their focus between us. My mind scrambled for a way to draw out the confusion as long as I could. Then I caught sight of Dune.

He approached us at a run, grabbing me and pulling me away from Mom and the rips.

"Don't give in, Hallie."

He put his body between the rips and me.

It worked.

They were staring only at my mother now, and she gaped at them in horror. They began to circle her, and I held on to Dune instead of being absorbed into the lives of those already dead.

"Can you get us out?" he asked.

I'd have to make a choice.

I stared at my mother, who even now was trying to wave the rips in my direction.

I took Dune's hand and closed the rip world.

I left my mother behind.

My hair was still wet from the shower when I climbed into his lap, which was my new favorite place. If we had to be vertical. "She'll get out. She's not activated. She doesn't have enough strength to sustain them."

He held me close, and his big hand ran slow circles over my back. "Are you okay?"

"At least I know the truth now."

"Do you want to talk about it?" he asked.

I wanted to call my dad, see if he'd known the truth, any part of it. "Not right now. Right now let's talk about how you got this scar." I smoothed my finger over his eyebrow.

"I fell off the kitchen counter when I was three."

"Why were you on the kitchen counter?"

"I was trying to get glue off the top of the fridge so I could attach my Matchbox cars to the coffee table."

"I bet you were a mess of a toddler." And got away with everything. No mother would've been able to resist those eyes. "Do you have siblings?"

"Three. Two of them own a kick-ass resort on the Kona coast. Obviously, I've never been to visit. The other is in med school at USC."

"You're the baby?"

"Yep."

I tickled him, hoping he'd tickle back, because that got his hands near the places I wanted them. When he didn't, I kissed him and slid my hands up the back of his shirt.

"Hallie. We need to talk about today. I don't want you to swallow the truth. It'll burn a hole through you."

"Why can't we act like everything is normal?" I removed my hands, put them in my lap. "Just for today?"

"Don't think I wouldn't rather be kissing you." He laid one on me that made my toes curl for posterity. "Because I would. But I'd also like to be kissing you next week and next month and next year. If we can't figure this out, that won't—"

"Next year." I leaned back to look at him. "You want to be kissing me next year?"

"Yes." Straight and true. "But you have to be here."

"You think there's a chance I won't be?"

When he didn't answer, I pushed away from him to go to the window. To calm my breathing. So I didn't have to see the truth on his face.

"You aren't the only one who loses if this situation goes wrong," he said. "I didn't see you coming, and then you were there, and now . . . you're everywhere."

"I never wanted to belong to someone." After Benny, I never wanted to risk loss like that again.

"You belong to yourself, Hal. More than anyone I've ever known."

"But I—I need you."

"You don't think I need you?" he asked.

I turned around to face him.

"I didn't come to New Orleans looking for this. I was trying to do a job, to carry my weight for the Hourglass. But now I've come to believe that my place is with you."

"Dune—"

"I'm going to be with you until we fix this. And I want to be with you after that." His shoulders raised and lowered. "All I need to know is what you want, and you don't have to tell me now, okay?"

"I already know," I said, crossing the room to him. "It's you."

Dune

Decorative pillows littered Hallie's bedroom floor the way confetti littered the city at Mardi Gras. At least the Mardi Gras I'd seen.

"How long do you think we can hold Mom off once she gets out of the rip?" Hallie tucked her head in the crook of my shoulder.

Her hair was a mess again, and I realized how much I loved her like that. Breathless and ravished. Thanks to me.

"Since I'm assuming that at least half your determination comes from your mom, I don't expect her to take too long." I kissed her soundly and started picking up the cushions, tossing them to her one by one. "Hopefully, she thinks it's just you and me without backup. We need an advantage."

"I'm not sure she's anticipating a team of X-Men, but who knows?" She caught a pillow right in front of her face, and then peeked out from behind it, grinning. "Is Liam Ballard bald?"

"No, actually, but he's still more Professor X than Magneto."

"Speaking of hair," she said, "yours is a mess."

I looked in the mirror. I had enough hair for it to be a mess. "What day is it?"

"December tenth."

Christmas was a couple of weeks away. I felt like I'd known Hallie for years, but it wasn't enough. She stepped up beside me, and we looked at our side-by-side reflection. My skin was tan, hers was pale. We both had light eyes and dark hair, but her features were delicate. Mine were big and broad.

"I like the way we look," she said, meeting my eyes.

"I concur."

"I've been waiting to give you my Christmas wish list, and I think this is the perfect time."

"Because we have the opportunity to shop right now?" I faced her, smoothed her messy hair. "Kidding. Spring it on me."

"Spend Christmas here. With me. That's all. That's the only thing I want."

The statement was reminiscent of what she'd said to me on the stairs the day she'd threatened to get me fired. Forever ago. "I thought the only thing you wanted was to know my name."

The kiss she gave me was sweet. "I knew you'd catch that."

A knock interrupted the moment. Hallie opened the door to Michael and Em. They both looked serious.

"Any word on Teague?" Michael asked. His eyes widened, like he was trying to communicate something silently.

"Not yet," Hallie said, looking back and forth between us, pulling her hair into a knot on top of her head.

"Hallie, can I borrow you for a second?" Emerson asked. "I wanted . . . I needed you to . . ."

"Talk to me alone so that Michael will stop doing the eyebrow-raise thing, and he and Dune can have a private conversation?" Hallie asked.

Em let out a sigh. "Thank you."

Grinning, Hallie stood on her tiptoes to kiss me. I gave her one last squeeze. Michael followed me downstairs to the living room.

"Sit." I gestured toward the couch.

He rubbed his hand over his face. "I've been reading through the Infinityglass research, the part you told me to focus on. I talked to Liam, too. This isn't a sit-down conversation."

I disagreed. Michael was pacing, and it made my stomach threaten an out-of-body experience. I sat.

"If you follow it to its logical conclusion, transmutation is about cell regeneration. Regeneration, making things new. Renewal. Fixing what's broken."

"I understand the definition. Hallie does, too."

Being a smart-ass wasn't in my wheelhouse, so Michael let the comment go. "Regeneration, especially if it happens that fast, could heal the continuum."

"What are you saying?" I asked.

"I believe Hallie could heal the continuum."

"You think she has enough power to do that?" I heard the strain in my own voice, felt the kick in my gut.

"If the rips continue to possess her and she continues to fight them, she'll eventually burn out." He shoved his hands in his back pockets. "The Skroll info proves the Infinityglass was never meant to bear a load like this. Healing individual rips could've been manageable, possibly her purpose. Crowds of them, no. Entire rip worlds, no."

His words echoed in my head.

"I agree with your theory. They possess her because they want to live through her," he continued. "But they want more than that. They want her to fix them."

I stared at him as things from the Skroll shuffled into place. Information I hadn't understood in the context of an object. "The amount of regenerated cells she produces could heal the rifts in the continuum."

"Only if she's inside it." Michael's eyes clouded with concern. "The rips are multiplying; their worlds are taking over. Time is ripping apart around us, Dune, and Hallie might be the only one who can repair it."

She could repair it.

But could she survive it?

Chapter 21
Hallie

"*I* am super awkward at social situations in general, and there's some major stuff going down, so I'm not going to hold to any sort of societal standard, and I'm just going to pretend like we've known each other long enough to say what's on our mind, and I hope that's okay." Emerson blurted all of this out in the ten seconds after the door shut behind her.

"You are intense." Maybe she was overcompensating for height, like Napoleon and his complex.

"I am."

"And you aren't apologizing for it. I really, really admire that." My phone buzzed an alert. I was supposed to have called Dad, but got distracted by Dune. "Crap."

"Everything okay?" Emerson asked, and then she covered her mouth with one hand. "I mean, obviously, everything isn't okay. I was referring to the 'crap.' That you said. When you said, 'crap.'"

I laughed, deep and long, and realized I hadn't in a while. "I'm kind of wondering where you've been all my life."

"Um, committed. At least for part of it." Emerson frowned. "That sounds scary, out of context."

This girl was so authentic she probably had a trademark stamped on her ass.

"So explain it. And do you mind if I stretch? I get antsy after the possessions." Talk about things that sounded scary out of context.

"Go for it." She sat down on the edge of my bed, and I sat down on the floor and started with my hamstrings. I moved through two sets of stretches, but she wasn't talking.

"I can stretch and listen at the same time." I rested my forehead on my knees.

"Right. It's just, wow. You are really . . . bendy."

"That's what three dance classes a week will do for you. Usually, anyway. It's been a busy week." I shot her a look and felt very gratified when she laughed. "On with the story."

"My parents died in an accident. To keep it short, I've existed in two time lines. One involves me being burned horribly in over forty percent of my body. Skin grafts to my back. Medications. Pain. Debilitating depression to the point of institutionalization." She cleared her throat. "And then there's the time line where Jack Landers screwed with my life."

"I thought Jack took memories and then ran around trying to find out how to be all-powerful by using them against people."

I stretched my neck to the right and then to the left.

"He might sound small-time, but he's not. Jack's time line saved me from the accident, but it was so he could use me. For his nefarious purposes." Forced humor distorted her voice. "Nothing like owing your life to a madman."

I stopped stretching. "I didn't know. I'm sorry—"

"Don't apologize, Hallie, please. I didn't explain for sympathy; I just like people to know where I'm coming from. Keeps things from getting complicated."

"Do you still struggle with the depression?"

"It's manageable," she confessed. "But I have bad days."

"Since we're being honest." I took the opportunity to lighten things up by morphing my features. First into Lily's and then into Emerson's, before restoring my own.

"I just saw . . . my face . . . on your face. I might . . . need to go throw up."

I laughed. "I promise to never do it again. I'm just saying that I want people to know where I'm coming from, too."

"We were all shocked when we found out you and Dune were . . . um, whatever it is that you are." She took that moment to focus on a pair of Dune's jeans on my floor.

"Uh . . . yeah." I looked up at my ceiling fan.

"Right. Okay. Well. Good, then." She cleared her throat. "I like you, and I can see why he likes you, too. He's always been kind and smart, but, Hallie, he's a different person around you."

"I didn't think good relationships were supposed to change

people." I'd never seen one make a person better. Not before I'd met the Hourglass crew.

"Who told you that? That's their purpose. You make him strong." She lifted her chin. "Michael does that for me."

"What was Dune like before?" I'd been dying to ask someone, and Emerson was too honest not to dish.

"A lot like he is now, but less . . . in control. It's not that he was out of control at the Hourglass—there just weren't a lot of opportunities for him to lead. He seems older now."

"Michael does the leading in Ivy Springs?"

"Yup." She smiled, and I recognized pride. "He's good at it."

"My life has been pretty sheltered. I've had to learn how to be strong on my own. Dune is like . . . a partner. He makes it easier for me to just be."

"How?"

I frowned.

"You don't have to explain, unless you want to."

I couldn't stop my smile. "I think I do."

"Well, then." She dropped down onto the floor and folded her legs into a pretzel shape. "Tell me *all* about it."

"It was fun at first, teasing him. But he handled it, and I barely shook him. Well, maybe I did that time I almost flashed him."

Emerson's jaw dropped a little.

"I'd only known him for a week, so . . . anyway. No one's ever been able to keep up with me. No one's tried. Then there was

Dune, and all that—*presence*—and then he's so sweet, especially his—"

"Eyes! I know." Emerson grinned. "But don't tell Michael I know."

"Our secret." I grinned back at her. I could get used to a girl-friend. "He doesn't make any demands on me. He listens, pays attention to what I'm actually saying, and responds to that. He's amazing."

She had a smug look on her face. "I knew it. I even told Michael."

"Told him what?"

"This is the real thing."

I didn't know what to say to that or whether to address it at all, so I changed the subject. "What did Michael want to talk to Dune about?"

Em's smugness disappeared. "He found something on the Skroll. He wouldn't tell me what."

"That means it's serious," I said.

"Probably."

"Then I say it's time we crash the party."

Dune

Hallie and Em had just come downstairs when Kaleb and Lily entered through the kitchen. They all found seats and looked at me.

"What's going on?" Hallie asked as she looked around. "Must be pretty big if we're about to have a group conversation."

"It's a group problem." I didn't waste any time. "It's about the rip situation, and the fact that every time you're possessed, you're cycling through an enormous number of cells."

"Supernatural exfoliation. It's really great for the complexion," Hallie deadpanned. She went pale when no one even cracked a smile. "Okay. Why does this nugget of information require a powwow?"

"All the energy from the cells you create is the same thing that allows you to close the rifts in time. That energy could transfer to the space time continuum. We think you can heal it."

"I'm all in. What do I have to do?" Hallie asked.

I wished I could let the hope shining on her face last for more than thirty seconds. "It's not that simple. So far, you've managed to close the rips while you were outside them."

Anxiety clouded her expression again in the shape of a frown. "I have to go inside a rip to close it."

"We don't know anything for certain," I explained. "We don't even know if it will work."

"But it could." She sat on the edge of the coffee table. "If I had the power to undo all the damage that's been done, the rip worlds would go away."

Michael nodded. "That's what we think."

Footsteps thundered down the stairs. Poe swung into the living room holding a notebook, stopping in front of Hallie, his face haggard. "It's my fault. I'm the one who activated you."

"What are you talking about?" She stood and reached for Poe's arm. "Sit down. You look terrible."

"I finally found the answer on the Skroll." He shook her off and kept talking. "At first, I thought something we stole kicked you off. Something you'd touched on a job or even someplace we'd been. But it was me. I did it. The night I pulled you into the veil and teleported you."

"You teleported Hallie?" I asked.

"No one is supposed to go in veils but time travelers and teleporters." Kaleb was talking to Poe without meeting his eyes. No love lost between those two.

"It was a do-or-die situation." Poe didn't look at him either. He didn't look at anyone but Hallie. "And my fault."

"Stop," Hallie said.

Kaleb wasn't going to let it go. "You never told us what your exotic matter source is. You have to have it to open veils. How are you teleporting yourself or anyone else?"

"I create my own exotic matter."

"Can other people use it, too?" Emerson asked. "Like, say, time travelers?"

Dead quiet descended on the room. Cat Rooks, Hourglass's source of exotic matter, had betrayed us. No one with the time travel skill had been able to use it since she walked out.

"I think they can." Poe's attention shifted from Hallie to Emerson, and then to Michael.

Michael nodded, and Emerson took his hand.

From the way Kaleb looked at Poe, he'd discovered some affection for him. "The night you killed Emerson, I couldn't get a pinky toe into the veil. It was as hard as a rock."

"I'm sorry, what?" Hallie stared at Kaleb as if he'd claimed his life goal was to be a princess.

"Oh." Em waved her hands at Hallie like it was no big deal. "There was this time that Poe killed me, but it totally didn't stick, and we've worked it out. So. Don't worry about it."

Hallie's eyes were wide. "I'm worried."

"I wasn't operating under my own volition." Poe's face went dark, shuttering any emotion.

"He's apologized, numerous times." Em smiled at him. "Then after that, he saved me and Michael."

"It's not like I'm a hero," Poe said, but his expression lightened. "But I hope I've found another way to make it up to you both."

"You're a hero to us, Poe." Hallie looked at Poe until he met her eyes. "Always will be."

"I hate to ruin the moment, but can we bring the focus back around to Hallie?" I waited until I had everyone's attention. "Poe managed to pull you in, and you survived."

"Because of her regeneration ability," Poe said. "Has to be."

"I was so sick that night," Hallie said, her gaze intensifying. "I came out on the other side, couldn't hear or see, and I kept throwing up. That was the night I saw a rip for the first time, but Poe saw it, too, so I didn't suspect anything or connect the dots. The next day was when my regeneration went into overdrive."

"I'm so sorry, Hallie." Poe stared at her, and the darkness was back.

"Do *not* apologize to me, or blame yourself for this."

"But—"

"But shut up." She grabbed Poe's shoulders and leaned in close. "You aren't responsible. Did you do it on purpose?"

Poe shook his head.

Hallie squeezed him before letting go and facing the group, hands on hips, chin angled out. "It wasn't Poe's fault."

"We agree with you, Hallie," Michael said quietly.

"That's it. That's the answer." My brain spun so fast my vision was blurry. I sat down to get my bearings and to take control of the hope in my chest. "If the veil was the stressor that set Hallie off, then Poe could pull Teague into a veil and set off her activation."

"How do you feel about that?" Emerson asked Hallie, in a soft voice.

"If we did it on purpose?" Emotions raced across Hallie's face. "It doesn't make me any different from her. She created me as a tool, and now my ticket out is using her as one?"

Teague had never treated Hallie like a mother should treat a daughter. Even the bedtime stories she'd told Hallie had an ulterior motive.

"She could help you with the rips. Maybe it would confuse them, like it did in the park. Maybe it would slow them down." I pushed up off the couch. "You can't expect me to choose between her comfort and yours. There's no universe where this even comes close to a contest."

"It's not just about her comfort, or the rips. If she's activated, she could heal the continuum. She could go in and not come out."

"We don't know if that's even a valid answer to the problem," I argued. "Are you just supposed to fight the rips by yourself when you could have help?"

"Help from her comes with a price. It always has, and that won't change now." Tears formed in her eyes.

When I reached out for her, she pulled away. "Hallie, think about this logically, please."

"I can't . . . I just . . . I have to think." Hallie turned away from me and picked up her phone. "I have to make a call."

And then she was gone.

Chapter 22
Hallie

The sliding glass door opened as soon as I hung up.

"Can I join you?" It was Kaleb.

"Sure." I put down my phone and wiped my eyes before facing him. I figured the first place people would look was my studio, so I'd escaped to the pool.

"I wanted to talk to you about a couple of things," he said.

"That's worrisome. Have a seat."

He sat down beside me on the concrete as I sized him up. The dimples, the baby blues, the body. If I'd seen him in the Quarter, cruising Bourbon three months ago, I'd have had him pressed up against the back corner of a bar in fifteen minutes or less. Now? Nothing.

He tried to stop a grin, but couldn't manage it.

"Damn." I turned eight shades of eggplant. "I forgot you could read minds."

"Not minds. Emotions." He reached out to swirl his hands in the water. "Water is actually one of the ways I tune them out. But I have to be submerged."

"Well, go ahead and dive in, because I don't want to know what you just got from me."

"No need. I got the same thing you'd get from me. We could've done some serious damage together at some point and time. But we're where we're supposed to be." He acknowledged it as a fact and moved on, with no hint of flirtation or inappropriateness, passing the douche test with flying colors. "You're in love with Dune, or close at least. Have the two of you talked about it?"

There it was again, welling up like a spring. The fear of losing him. I shook my head.

"Don't let this overwhelm you," he admonished. "Nothing has happened. We can still beat it."

I stared down at my bright pink toenails in the water. "I bet you're a pain in the ass to be friends with."

"One of the best things about my ability is my excellent BS meter."

"I have one of those, too." I grinned. "Probably not as good as yours."

"There are people behind you who have your back."

"That's kind of new for me. My dad is overprotective, and my mom is just a sorry human altogether."

"We can't be responsible for the family life doles out to us. Jack Landers is my uncle."

"Damn."

"I heard you on the phone with your dad. Well"—he held up one finger—"that's not true. I felt you on the phone with your dad. That's why I came down."

"Our relationship is . . . difficult."

"My dad was dead."

I jerked my head around. "Was?"

"He's a time traveler. Explosions, continuum issues, search and rescue."

"The Hourglass seems to have a special talent for . . . bouncing back from death."

"True. But we've all had a rough year." He pointed to the tiny scars from previous piercings in his nose and eyebrow. The studs in his ears remained. "There are even war wounds."

I noticed the edges of a tattoo at his sleeve cuffs and collar. It made me think of Dune's, and the feel of his skin. Kaleb caught me staring. "Dune and I went to the tattoo parlor at the same time."

"I love his. I bet Lily likes yours."

"Lily accepts me for who I am. It took a long time, but so do I, and so does my dad. We're going to pull you through this. The Hourglass has a special talent for that, too."

I bit down on my lower lip. I didn't want any more waterworks.

As if Kaleb knew, he gave me a pat on the shoulder, stood, and left me to contemplate the steam rising off the water.

Dune

Kaleb told me I could find Hallie at the pool. When I'd stared at him for a few seconds, he'd told me I *should* find Hallie at the pool, and then he pushed me in the right direction.

I surprised her when I sat down.

"What are you doing?" She looked at the water like it was alive and ready to come out of the ground to swallow me whole.

My stomach crashed to my feet when I considered her motive for being where she was. "Did you come here because you hoped I wouldn't follow you?"

"No. No!" She grabbed my knee when I started to stand up. "I came outside barefoot without thinking about it, and the water is heated."

Logic, not purposeful avoidance.

We both leaned back, hands behind us. Hallie's feet were in the pool, mine folded uncomfortably. She gave me a side glance, and I turned around, back to the water, legs stretched out in front of me. We were still shoulder to shoulder, but I liked this position better. I could look at her face.

"There's a pool outside the Hourglass. I actually *live* in the pool house." I grinned. "How's that for irony?"

"I'm glad pools don't bother you." She gave me a shoulder bump. "I bet you play a mean game of chicken, and we need to incorporate pool time into our first vacation together."

"First vacation?" I watched her expression closely. "Does that mean you've reached a decision about how to handle the rip situation?"

"I talked to my . . . dad."

That explained why she'd grabbed her phone and run outside so quickly, and was probably the reason why Kaleb had followed shortly thereafter.

"What did he say?"

"He agrees with your plan, thinks she should share the load. He wanted to drop everything and come home."

"Did you think he wouldn't?" I asked.

"I have a lot to think about. I asked him to trust me."

"I'm sorry that it's come to this, but the choice is crystal clear to me."

"There's a part of me, a really stupid part, that still wishes things could be different. That she'd be the cookie-baking mom, the kind that was a hundred percent in my corner. But I know that's not the case, and it never will be." She took a deep breath. "And Dad used to love her. I asked him if he knew about the genetic engineering. He said he didn't. He also said he didn't love her anymore."

"Is he your—"

"Yes." Her conviction was accompanied by calm. "In every way that matters, and biologically. She didn't pick my dad to be her husband by accident."

"I'm sorry you had to find out this way."

"I'm not. It's one of the best things she did. Maybe the best."

"It resulted in you." I leaned in, and then stopped a millimeter away. She closed the distance.

It was a slow kiss. I savored her mouth, concentrating on it and nothing else. I wanted us to live our lives in seconds instead of hours, because no one knew how many we had left.

"There are too many people in this house," she murmured against my lips.

"So let's get a plan together and get rid of them."

She pulled away. "Do you have ideas?"

My gaze traveled the length of her body. "So many."

I got an eye roll, but she didn't mean it. "About the rips?"

"I think so." I stood up and held out my hand. "Your mom is out there somewhere, and I'd rather we find her than vice versa."

She put her feet on the ground and let me help her up. Once she was standing, I turned around. "Piggyback?"

"Piggyback?"

"Yeah. I don't want your toes to get cold."

She put her arms around my neck and jumped. When her legs went around my waist, I wrapped my hands around her feet and started for the house.

"Dune?"

Her breath was warm on the back of my neck. "Yeah?"

"I'm falling in love with you."

I didn't miss a step. "Good. Because I'm already there."

Chapter 23
Hallie

After Dune's breathing was deep and even, I slipped out of bed. I was too nervous to read, and listening to music only made me want to dance, which wasn't conducive to other people's sleeping patterns. I was supposed to contact my mother the next morning and ask her to meet us at Poe and Dune's apartment, where Poe would pull her into a veil.

Poe had disappeared after agreeing to the plan. I'd tried to talk to him, to make sure he knew that whether he helped or not was his choice, and that he shouldn't feel pressured. He'd just shaken his head and walked away, carrying blame on his back like fully stacked free weights.

I stared out the window at my studio, my usual solace in times of stress, and grabbed my toe shoes. I slipped downstairs and outside in less than a minute. I'd just passed the courtyard when the bottom dropped out.

The wrought iron gate made a clanging sound, and I stopped dead.

"Hallie! Get down!"

Carl, head of security, had followed me out of the house. I remained frozen as he lurched toward me. The sound of a silenced gunshot echoed three times, and he clutched his chest and hit the ground.

Memories broke free from my subconscious. Benny's blue eyes, wide open and empty. The devastating feeling that it was my fault.

The blood.

It covered the pavers now, just as it had covered the gray stones outside Jackson Square. The difference was that Carl still had light in his warm brown eyes, and he was talking to me. I dropped to the ground beside him.

"Run. Your dad will never . . . forgive . . ."

"I'm not leaving you." I searched the dark, hoping for help, but fearing more violence. "Someone heard the shots, they had to—"

My head jerked back as a hand wrapped around my hair and pulled me to my knees. I looked up, expecting to see a guy holding a semiautomatic, some thug my father had crossed finally getting his revenge.

It was my mother, holding a handgun. A shadowy figure stood behind her, but I couldn't make out any features.

I stopped caring when two more shots fired, one to the back of each of my ankles.

Pain exploded through my Achilles tendons, and then everything went black.

Dune

Hallie was gone.

In an unthinking panic, I covered the whole house twice
before I thought to wake up Michael and Kaleb. "Hallie's gone.
None of the guards have seen her, and the lights are off in her
studio."

"I'll go get Lily. Hang tight, brother, and we'll find her." Kaleb
threw on clothes and headed for the girls' room.

Michael didn't inflict small talk on me while I waited. I paced.
My skin felt too small for my frame.

"Dune." Lily entered the room, followed by Kaleb. She had a
US atlas in her arms.

"Please tell me you found her."

"I did, but . . ."

When she hesitated, I growled, "Tell me."

"She's alive, and she was near the river. By the warehouses
behind the French Market."

"Who she's with?"

Lily bit her lip. "Her mother."

"Wait—you said she 'was' near the river. What does that
mean?" I asked.

"Now I think she's in it. They must be on a boat."

I cursed and punched my fist into the nearest wall. Teague had thrown my vulnerability in my face at the park, and now she was using it against me. What if Hallie encountered a rip world? What if she couldn't get out? My thoughts scrambled for purchase before finding a solid place to land. "Send Poe. He can get to her quick."

"Problem." Kaleb scrubbed his hand across his chin. "Poe is missing, too."

"Let me look for him." Lily opened the atlas and searched. "Nothing. It's not good, but it doesn't necessarily mean he's dead."

"He could be in a veil. That would keep Lily from being able to find him." Michael clapped a comforting hand on my shoulder. "Maybe he's already trying to find Hallie. Hang tight. We'll all go get dressed so we can head down to the wharf."

"Dune." Emerson appeared in the doorway, a blanket around her shoulders, tears in her eyes. "They found the head of security in the courtyard. He's been shot and he's on his way to the hospital. It doesn't look good."

My body went numb. Em was holding back. "What else?"

She crossed the room and put one hand on my arm. "It wasn't just Teague. Jack. And he didn't bother wiping Carl's memory. He . . . as he was going into the ambulance, Carl told us that Teague shot Hallie. Twice."

Emerson's tears streaked down her cheeks as she held

up a pair of toe shoes. They were splattered with blood.

"Meet me at the river." I took off at a run, and stopped briefly at the door to look back at Lily. "Keep ahold of that atlas. I'll call you for an update when I get there."

Chapter 24

Hallie

I woke up as the sun rose, opening my eyes to find seagulls wheeling above me.

Two levels of windows, plus an observation deck. The paint was a graying white, and the blue and yellow trim was mostly peeled away. Dull wood, dingy brass, and the smell of dead fish. A riverboat, its shipshape days long past.

There was an echoing pain in my ankles that wouldn't dull, even though the open wounds were healed. The irony that my mother had chosen my Achilles' heels wasn't lost on me.

Carl. She'd shot him. Who else had she hurt to get me here? Where was Dune?

Black, low-heeled boots echoed across the boat deck. Her apple red coat matched the color in her cheeks, and she should've painted a sunny picture. But the brightness in her eyes was menacing rather than cheerful.

"Hello, sunshine. Did you sleep well?"

"Bitch." I flexed my feet and groaned. "They'll find you."

"They might. I'm aware of what Lily can do. But Dune's the one you want, and he's going to think twice about the river."

"He'll handle the water." And if he couldn't, his friends could.

"Doesn't mean he'll find us. We're only hitching a ride." She curled her lip at our dilapidated surroundings. "There's a speedboat waiting a few miles away. Our next destination involves a lot of open water. It's difficult to pinpoint a location when you're always moving."

I felt my anxiety expand beyond the tightness in my chest and spread to the very corners of the ship, weaving its way through the railings and the wood, catching in the paddles at the stern. There were men on the ship, a crew of them. She'd been planning this.

A man wearing a tailored suit stood behind her. Not part of the crew.

"Oh, where are my manners?" Mom actually clucked. "Let me formally introduce Jack Landers."

Jack was so pale he was almost transparent. His eyes were dead in his face.

"Pleased to make your acquaintance." His overconfident tone suggested that he was used to getting what he wanted, and his slick smile told me the rest. A woman in a dirty yellow coat stepped out from the shadows.

Her nail-bitten fingers worried the buttons—open and closed, open and closed, over and over again. She didn't look at me, didn't even acknowledge where she was standing. Her eyes were vacant. Lost. She had to be strung out on something.

Jack ignored her and moved forward, leaning heavily on a cane, the smile growing wider. "I've waited a long time to meet you. I look forward to doing business with you."

"I can't say the same." Growing up in New Orleans taught me not to do deals with the devil. It was always a bitch when he came to collect.

Jack studied me. "What have they told you about me, Hallie?"

"You manipulate people to get what you want." I rolled to a sitting position, wincing when I tried to stand and couldn't. My ankles weren't ready, and I felt too vulnerable on the ground. "I'm guessing you're responsible for whatever's wrong with her."

He looked at the woman beside him. "I haven't done anything she didn't ask me to do."

"You steal memories, and she doesn't look like she can remember her own name." The woman stared vacantly in the direction of the shore. Flecks of spittle gathered at the corners of her mouth. "Did she ask for that?"

"She asked me to make life better for her, which involved erasing some things she wanted to forget. It took a while, since there were a lot of . . . situations to work through." The two of them came closer. Her hair was short and unkempt, and she couldn't focus on anything for more than a few seconds. "However, erasing you from the memories of your new friends shouldn't be too difficult. Erasing all of them from *your memory* might be."

The hair on the back of my neck stood straight up. If being erased resulted in the ruin of the woman standing in front of me, screw my aching ankles. It was time to start running. I tried standing again.

"You think they're your friends, but they'll forget you easily. They're all so malleable." Jack looked at my mother. "Does Hallie know Lily told us where to find the pendant? On Halloween, when I 'borrowed' her from the Hourglass."

My chest tightened at the thought of Lily doing anything to help Jack or my mother. "What pendant?"

Jack answered for her. "Obviously, your mother never needed to search for the Infinityglass. But she did need the thing that allowed the Infinityglass to transfer abilities."

I made it as far as one knee and one foot on the floor. "I don't believe for one second that Lily would help you find it."

"Lily didn't know. Still doesn't. We made her think it was a simple location test, so I didn't even have to wipe her memory. Tell me." Jack leaned over conspiratorially. "Does Emerson like you? I hope she does. She's already so fractured. If she's formed an attachment, erasing you from her mind will take her one step closer to where I need her."

His eyes held a sick elation. I wondered how someone could be happy about causing so much pain, and then I thought about the things Jack had done to Emerson. Changed her time line, erased her memories. Her words came back to punch me in the solar plexus.

"Nothing like owing your life to a madman."

If Jack kept going, would he rob her of the happiness she had now? Would she end up mindless and empty, too?

Jack was too pleased with the sound of his own voice to shut up for long. "Dune will be harder. He loves you, and that just makes it all the more tragic. Because if he or your father gives us trouble, we'll take care of them the same way we took care of Gerald Turner."

Even though I was still on the floor, I lost my equilibrium. I put my palms flat as my vision blurred. When it cleared, I stared up at my mother. Not an ounce of emotion crossed her face.

"How is it that you haven't given Jack 'trouble'?" I asked. "Why hasn't he taken your memories?"

"I know how to block him. He's the one who taught me how, back when we were both in Memphis."

Jack looked like he regretted the choice.

"Too bad she didn't learn the trick." I gestured to the woman beside Jack. "Whoever she is."

"I'll introduce you." He took my arm and hauled me to my feet. "Cat, you're being rude. Shake hands with Hallie."

Cat stared at Jack for a long moment.

He nodded, and she made a grab for my hand.

My very bones vibrated the second she touched me. Time slowed down, my body roaring as if an electrical fire burned under my skin. Something that felt like a rectangular piece of metal branded the skin below my collarbone.

"Let go," I screamed over the sound of the wind in my ears and tried to jerk my arms free, but got nowhere. "Let me go. . . ."

Cat's mouth formed an O shape as her skin tightened on her already skeletal face. I was draining her energy. I felt it flowing through me. To Jack. His hand was still on my arm.

All the noise and activity dissipated in a rush. I hit the ground again.

Cat followed.

A mere husk of the woman lay crumpled in a heap. After-shocks of power surged through me, but I ignored them and put my fingertips on her throat, searching. She looked like an addict who'd taken things too far. Desperate, starving, ruined.

Dead.

Jack held a spinning purple sphere in his hands. It gave off a crazy, glowing light, and crackled with electricity, just as I had thirty seconds ago. I'd seen Poe with something similar. Exotic matter.

"It worked," Jack crowed, mesmerized. "She transferred Cat's ability to me."

Whether Cat had been willing or not, she'd overdosed on Jack Landers and his ability to take away pain. He had been her illicit drug.

I looked at the dead body beside me and wondered if he was about to make me his next addict.

Dune

I hadn't underestimated the power of the Mississippi. Muddy, churning, and teeming with life, the current pulsed strong and willful. The closer I got to its banks, the more it pulled at me. Regulating my intake of air was the first step to maintaining control, the second, exhaling.

The desire to see what I could do was powerful, flowing through my veins faster than my blood. The desire to keep Hallie alive was stronger.

The cab dropped me off just below the Port of New Orleans, and I followed the coordinates Lily had texted me. They led to a docked riverboat. I could see Hallie lying on the deck. Jack Landers stood beside her, holding a spinning ball of exotic matter in his hands.

The loading dock was at the other end of the boat. I approached it at a run, slowing down as I crossed it, and only then to soften the sound of my footsteps.

Chapter 25
Hallie

*F*ast as a snap, Jack lost twenty years. His pale hair brightened to blond, and his skin glowed with color. His cane hit the ground, and he left it where it fell.

"Exotic matter. First step, complete." Jack tossed the light up, and then mimicked hitting it with a bat. It shot out like a home run, highlighting a veil behind him.

Mother waved to a couple of men by the paddle wheel and gestured for them to pull in the loading dock. No one could get on or off the boat without it, even though we were still tethered to shore, which meant I was on my own.

"You have what you wanted," she said. "I'm sure it's all you hoped for."

My stomach roiled with the consequences. We'd known the Infinityglass could possibly transfer powers between people with time-related abilities, but we'd focused on dealing with the rips.

"It's all we hoped for," Jack said.

I started a slow crab walk backward. Jack was beside me in seconds, hauling me up by the arm. "You aren't going anywhere."

"Don't make me do that again." I felt like crying, but I didn't want to show Jack an ounce of weakness. "I won't."

"You will, because that's your purpose." He steered me to a bench by the ship's railing. "I have records. Years of information about people with time-related abilities. You're just one of the tools I need to possess them all."

"One of the tools *we* need," Teague said, the mocking tone slight, but present. "Right, Jack?"

"What are the others?" I asked.

She pointed to my neck. I reached up to find the pendant I'd noticed her wearing in Audubon Park.

"There's nothing standing in the way now. We have everything we need," Jack said, beaming at my mother.

My mother smiled in return. Jack didn't know her well enough to understand what a smile like that meant, but I did.

"Not everything. You've forgotten something very important, Jack."

"I didn't forget—" He faltered, sensing something amiss in her expression. "But . . . I helped you find the pendant."

"You participated, but you didn't discover what activates an Infinityglass, and if you remember, that was part of our deal."

"I can still find out. We have endless resources now, and a way to use them, thanks to you." As he tried to wheedle his way into her good graces, I wondered how long she'd had him whipped.

"Maybe I already know." Her words slipped over me like cold silk. "But if you ever do, you'll have a weapon to use against me. One I can't block."

She waited. Let it sink in. Everything about his demeanor proved he hadn't anticipated the double cross. Then she made her move.

The amount of energy Mom pulled from him was double what I'd experienced when Jack had used me to drain Cat. I was now transferring two abilities, his and Cat's, to my mother's body. The current ran through me again, and the same pain seared my skin under the pendant. In addition to the burst of electricity, flashes of memory crowded my brain: a crying girl, with auburn hair and brown eyes; Poe, with a knife to his throat; a little boy, running into the path of a car.

Grief, anger, terror, and then it was done. I slumped back onto the bench as Mother gave Jack a hard shove. He pitched over the railing into the river.

Dead before he hit the water.

Dune

Jack Landers left no legacy other than a wake of destruction. Teague brushed his touch off her coat and forgot he ever existed in the same breath. The Hourglass's biggest perceived threat had been nothing but a pawn.

Hallie pointed to something around her neck. I slid closer to her and Teague, keeping my back to the main cabin, grateful the crew was busy making preparations to launch.

"You were wearing this the other day. What does it do?" Hallie asked her mother.

"It's duronium. If your skin is exposed to the pendant for an extended period of time, it reacts with your body chemistry and serves as a conductor. Creates the connection between those who have time abilities. Whoever you touch first receives the ability."

"Or whoever touches me first." Hallie dropped the pendant. "You had on a turtleneck at the park, which means you were afraid to let it out of your sight, but smart enough not to let it touch your skin. It's not like I don't have access to duronium. Poe's knife. Weren't you afraid I'd conduct too soon?"

"Maybe an Infinityglass requires this particular piece." Teague shrugged. "Or maybe I assumed any prolonged exposure to Poe's knife would result in your death. But only on my orders."

"I don't take your orders. I'm not a killer." In one swift movement, Hallie grabbed the pendant and jerked down, but the chain didn't break free. A red line marked her neck, and blood welled below it.

"I didn't ask you to be. I'll leave the killing to Poe," Teague said. "You're nothing but a weapon now."

As long as Hallie wore that pendant, she was untouchable, just another way for her mother to isolate her.

My mind raced to find an answer. Poe's exotic matter had been necessary to get Teague in a veil, but thanks to Cat, Teague had her own. Poe's duronium knife had factored in, too, but Hallie had duronium hanging around her neck. And what had Teague meant about leaving the killing to Poe?

I scanned the river. A veil shimmered a few hundred yards downstream.

I measured the pull of the tethers against the dock. Studied the flow of the current. Considered the trajectory of the vessel when it launched.

I had one tiny, miniscule chance to turn things around.

But I'd need the river's help.

Chapter 26
Hallie

"For the amount of intellect that man had, you'd think he would've anticipated that outcome."

Two people just died at my hand. My own mother made me an accessory to murder.

"Greed makes people blind and dumb." I offered. "Or maybe he didn't know you well enough to understand that your go-to is betrayal."

"I've never betrayed you, Hallie."

"You betrayed me before I was ever born."

"I created you for a unique purpose. Picked every single trait."

"I'm another version of you, Mother dear. Created to resemble the creator. You even gave me a calling. Sound familiar?"

She was so busy buying her own propaganda that she didn't even hear me. "I always wanted to dance as a child, but we didn't live close enough to a studio for me to walk to classes. I picked that for you."

"Did you cause my accident, too?" It was sarcasm, not an accusation.

But she blinked.

My knees grew weak and threatened to give. "Did you have something to do with Benny's death?"

Mother stared over my head. "The guard wasn't supposed to follow you. You wouldn't have been hurt if he hadn't tackled you."

"Benny was my best friend."

"He was an attachment you didn't need."

"He was my friend and I loved him." Long-buried grief surged in my heart. "That's the way humans are supposed to work. I tried to love you."

And I deserved to be loved.

"Love is a nice concept, but ultimately life is about the survival of the fittest, and who's strong enough to come out on top."

"You never should've been a parent. Thank God I had Dad."

"How do you think your father will feel when he finds out you were a means to an end?"

"He already knows." I lifted my chin. "And his love is more than enough to make up for what a piss-poor mother you've been."

She smirked. "What about Dune? Because I've seen the way you two look at each other, and that's not love."

"Yes, it is." She couldn't shake my faith in him, in us. He'd said it and he'd showed me. He came to New Orleans and stayed. Stuck by me when the crazy started. Called in his friends to serve as backup. Offered me a piggyback ride, because he didn't want my toes to get cold. "He gave up his life to help me."

"The Infinityglass is an obsession for him. He came for *it*, not you."

"It seems like you're trying to convince me that you're a more appealing option than he is. You created me in a lab, not out of love. You want me to murder for you. You've got the Infinityglass gene. Why can't you do it yourself?"

"I don't want to be a tool."

"So you built one. The Infinityglass is vulnerable because you believe the true power lies with the person who controls it." The truth got uglier. "I am your daughter. Do you have any concept of what family is supposed to mean?"

She ignored the question. "Get in the cabin."

"Are you going to make me forget about my life here? Daddy? Dune? How long would it take you to turn me into Cat? Because that's what you'll end up with if you expect me to go with you without a fight."

"What I expect is for you to get in the cabin. I still have the gun. My next shot might involve an artery. I don't know how quickly your cells can regenerate, but I imagine the healing process would be painful, especially if you had to do it repeatedly."

There had to be another option. I wouldn't kill for her again. I scanned the shore. Too far to jump, and too many bodies in the way.

"Don't even think about it. You can't get past the crew unless you can fly, and they won't hesitate to fish you out of the water."

"Whatever did you do to make an entire ship of sailors so loyal to you?" I smiled sweetly as the implication landed exactly where I'd aimed.

She didn't get a chance to answer.

"Hey, boss!" One of the men waved and held up a satellite phone. "Port authority question before we shove off."

She turned her back on me and signaled to one of the deckhands. He crossed over to Cat, picked up her body, and tossed her into the water.

I watched the proud line of my mother's posture as she walked away, and thought that I'd rather give myself over to the rips than let her control me for the rest of my life. It was an option. One to consider, eventually. I wasn't ready to give my life up yet.

Movement by the cabin caught my eye, and my heart became a rapid bass line thumping in my chest. Rips, as if they'd read my mind. How would I fight them on my own?

I turned around.

Not rips.

Dune.

Dune

If I made one misstep, I could unleash the power of the Mississippi and kill us all.

Water. Nothing but molecules—hydrogen and oxygen atoms. The compound that made up more than half of every human on the planet, including me. Liquid matter that could bend to my will. My will.

I focused on exactly where the veil hung in the atmosphere.

"Dune. Dune!"

Hallie.

I held a finger up to my lips. Teague was too far away to hear Hallie's whispers, but I didn't want to take any chances.

"You're on a boat," she whispered. "In the river. And you're fine. How?"

"Because *you're* on a boat in the river, and I have to be fine to help you get back to dry land."

Her eyes softened, and in that moment, I wanted to touch her more than I wanted to breathe.

"Hal, I have an idea, but we don't have a lot of time, so you have to trust me."

"Tell me what to do."

"Don't look at me, for starters."

She focused on the dock as I briefly explained the plan. "I'm going to try to guide Teague into a veil using the river."

271

Hallie's eyes went wide. "You're going to use your ability."

"I don't see any other options, and I'm going to need your help. Teague has Cat's exotic matter. I need you to try to get the necklace off. It's the missing ingredient to get her into the veil."

"I'll try." She straightened, and I flattened myself out against the side of the cabin seconds before Teague said her name.

"Hallie. Why aren't you in the cabin?"

"I want to say a melancholy good-bye to my childhood home. Not that you understand why, because that would require emotion."

Hallie stepped away from the railing. That was my cue.

I breathed in and out and called the current. It complied with a slight shift toward the opposite bank.

Adjusting things too fast could cause an accident. As it stood, it was only a matter of time before one of the deckhands noticed me.

I tried not to think about the day, all those years ago, when I had asked the ocean for help and it gave me the wrong answer. Hallie stood on the boat deck, five feet away from her mother.

I couldn't mess this up.

I tried again, shifting the flow a little more this time. Not enough. The crewmen had already begun to loosen the moorings. Stern, midship, and bowline.

Teague wasn't in position, and Hallie was still trying to take off the pendant.

I closed my eyes to concentrate and gave the current one more nudge.

"Stop! No!"

Hallie, in trouble. My eyes flew open, expecting an out-of-control rip. Instead, I saw Teague staring at me. Fury flashed across her face, quickly replaced by cunning. She grabbed Hallie's arm.

"Stay away from him." Hallie dug her heels into the deck. "Stop. I won't let you do this! I won't do this."

Teague became only more determined, yanking her daughter behind her.

Her intent was written all over her face. She was going to kill me, and she was going to use Hallie to do it.

Hallie

My mother lunged for Dune with determination and a grip that would leave bruises on my arm. I went limp to slow her down.

That's when a rip of a woman in a cancan costume stepped directly into our path. Mom lurched to the side to avoid it, and I broke free of her grasp and ran for Dune.

I exhaled the second he wrapped me in his arms. The relief and comfort that flooded through me felt like more than love. It felt like family.

"I can't get the pendant off. There must be a trick to the chain clasp."

He uttered a low oath. "It's soldered closed."

The development changed the plan, but gave us leverage. As long as I had the pendant around my neck and one hand on Dune, my mother wouldn't touch me. Too big of a risk for her to lose her powers and her life. But I didn't think anything would stop the rips. Their number only grew larger.

I faced her. "I see you've stopped in your tracks."

"I see you've forgotten about this." She held up the gun. "You can stand in front of him from here to Key West, but you can't stop a bullet."

I knew the words weren't empty.

"I'll go with you," I bargained. "We'll get on the speedboat and head to open waters and leave him here. You don't have to shoot him."

"You think he'll stop looking?"

"None of them will." From the look on Mom's face, she agreed.

He couldn't die. Not here. Not like this. Thanks to Jack Landers, there was another out.

"Don't kill him," I was reduced to whispering. "Erase him. Make him forget. He won't be a threat to you anymore."

She crooked a finger at the cabin. Someone had been inside the whole time. Listening. Watching.

Poe. Smiling at my mother.

Dune

I wanted to rip out Poe's heart and throw it and him to the bottom of the Mississippi. I hoped my face showed just how much. He was grinning, his posture relaxed.

A sharp whistle sounded on the other side of the deck. The moorings were stowed, and the riverboat pulled away from the dock. Poe's eyes stopped for one second on the veil that hung downriver as he walked toward Teague.

Hallie tensed in my arms as he passed, and I held her tighter.

"Well?" Poe stopped in front of Teague and crossed his arms over his chest. "You called your dog; he came."

"There are four members of the Hourglass in New Orleans. Hallie believes they'll look until they find her. You need to make sure that doesn't happen."

"Now?" Poe asked. "Or can I eat first?"

"How can you do this? Joke about it?" Hallie's voice broke. "Less than twenty-four hours ago, you were trying to—"

"Trying to what? Get in your pants? Oh no, wait. You're always the one trying to get in mine."

"Shut up." The growl came from deep in my chest, and my fists ached for Poe's face. "You apologize. Right now, you son of a—"

"It's okay." Hallie put her hand on my arm.

"No, it isn't," I argued, but I dialed down the testosterone.

"What the hell is wrong with you?" Hallie asked Poe. She had to raise her voice to be heard over the now churning paddle wheels. "You're supposed to be my best friend."

"Sweetheart, I'm your only friend. And what a sorry pair we are. Or were," he said, giving me the once-over. "As the case may be. Seems you've gone tropical."

I just smiled. He could insult me all he wanted, but if he breathed too close to Hallie, I was going to take him out.

"There's nothing wrong with me, Hallie. I survive. Good or bad, right or wrong, your mother is my best chance. It's not as bad as all that, is it? At least we'll be together." Turning to Teague, he said, "You want me to take out four, yeah?" He leaned over and slid his knife out of his boot.

Hallie shuddered.

Teague smiled. "All four."

"Who's here?"

"Kaleb, Lily, Michael, and Emerson."

"If I'd known I had to do Emerson again I'd have left her dead the first time I killed her." He turned away from Teague and walked toward the cabin, saluting us with his knife. "Not like I've ever been a hero to anyone, anyway. Least of all to you, Hallie."

And then he winked.

Hallie squeezed my forearm, but her expression didn't change. Poe hadn't switched sides. He was still on ours.

I looked downriver. We were still in line with the veil, the current following my subconscious bidding.

"You've taken care of the Hourglass," Hallie said. "What are you going to do about those?"

Teague looked toward the ever-growing population of rips. "Lots of room for history on a riverboat. Especially one this old."

Everything from Mark Twain types in white suits to tipsy senior citizens took up residence on the deck. I begged the heavens for a repeat of the rip in the park—that Hallie and Teague together would confuse the possession process.

My prayers were answered. The rips switched focus between Hallie and Teague. The riverboat chugged toward the veil. I wanted to boost the river flow, but I didn't know where Poe was, or how he planned on getting Teague where she needed to be. I would have to wait.

The rips didn't want to.

"Look at them." Hallie began to tremble. "They know who they want."

The rips moved in one accord, approaching Hallie at the same rate the riverboat approached the veil. I put my body between them, as if I could hide her from fate, but this time we couldn't run.

I wanted to call out for Poe, but I didn't want to tip Teague off about his allegiance, especially if something happened to me and Hallie was left on the boat with him. I looked over my shoulder. Too much was happening at once.

"Stay as close to me as you can," I said over my shoulder to Hallie.

Her breathing sped up. "If I go to them, she can't use me. She won't have any reason to hurt you or anyone else."

The rips were ten feet away.

The veil was fifteen.

"Hal, don't be reckless." Where was Poe?

"It's true, isn't it, Mother? You don't want to lose the Infinityglass, but you're afraid of the rips. What did you see when you were with them last? How did you manage to get away?"

Teague tore her gaze from the rips, which were now two feet away from Hallie.

The veil was right behind them.

I couldn't hold back the current any longer.

"Poe!" I tried to rein in the power of the water.

He burst out of the cabin with the knife in his hand.

"Throw it!" I roared. "Now!"

It left his hand in less than a second, tumbling end over end.

I set the current free.

Chapter 27

Hallie

The rips were coming for me, their pull terrifying and seductive. Impossible to resist.

The veil floated a few tantalizing feet away from my mother, but even though she had her own exotic matter, she didn't have duronium. Going with them was our only out. I'd just have to have faith that I'd come out on the other side.

And then Dune bellowed Poe's name.

His knife flew through the air, slicing its way into my mother's shoulder at the same time the veil swallowed her whole. She stumbled, gagging violently and clutching her head, her eyes rolling back.

As one, the rips swiveled their focus toward her.

Mother flew into the air as if jerked by an invisible string. Once there she floated, parallel to the ground. I would remember the look on her face for the rest of my life. Tears of furious defeat, and eyes wide with terror.

That's when I realized this possession was different.

Because she was still in the veil. Dune was holding the current steady.

Her body absorbed the rips, and not just their faces. Their bodies, too. We watched as they consumed her. Witnessed her skin melt away, heard her bones break, as she assumed each form.

Every single rip on the boat entered the veil, one by one, reshaping my mother into their images as they did. When they were gone, there was a flash of light and a terrible ripping sound. One keening scream.

Darkness devoured it all, including the veil, leaving behind nothing but the steady sound of paddle wheels churning up the Mississippi.

I stared at the empty air.

I wanted to feel sorry, feel *something*, but I was numb. Dune put his hand on my arm. "Hallie?"

Then Poe was in front of me, reaching out.

The consequences of one simple touch registered a second before it could happen.

"Stop!" I threw myself against the rail. "Don't touch me, either of you. Not until I get this necklace off."

How long would I have to worry about accidentally killing someone I loved?

"She made sure it wasn't going to come off easily. Fire's the only thing that's going to get through it." Poe held up his hands. "If you want, I can take care of that."

"Please." I voiced my other concern. "When will the duronium be out of my system?"

"It shouldn't take long, especially with your metabolism. You'll burn it off. Be right back."

Dune reached for me. In that second, I needed him to touch me more than I needed air in my lungs, but the fear of what I could've done by touching him or Poe weighed heavily.

"Just me," he said. "I'll move the second Poe comes back on deck."

I threw myself into his arms, burying my face in his chest, squeezing his waist. Safe. Solid. My anchor.

"I don't think she's coming out of the veil," I whispered, looking up at him.

The unusual sadness in his eyes told me he agreed. "I'm sorry for my part in it. I didn't know what would happen, but I wasn't expecting that. I can't stop thinking that it could've been you, Hallie. It could've been you."

"I know." My mother had been an unwilling sacrifice. That was going to take years to unpack, and trying to deal with it now was pointless. I would focus on the present. "Is everyone okay? Carl—"

"He was on his way to the hospital, and everyone else is fine."

Poe exited the cabin and conferred with one of the ship hands.

When he turned toward us, Dune let me go and took a step back.

"We're headed back to shore." Poe held up a tiny blowtorch. "Ready?"

"I'll check in with Michael," Dune said. "Be right back."

"Stay where I can see you." I sounded like his mom instead of his girlfriend, but I didn't care. Was I his girlfriend? The word seemed too simple.

Dune nodded. I should've known he'd understand.

"I'm sorry, Hallie." Poe shoved his free hand in his jeans pocket. "I don't know what else to say."

"How did you end up here?"

"Your dad asked for my help. That's why I was on the boat. When you made him promise not to come straight home, he called me. Thank God Teague still thought I was on her side."

I couldn't stop looking at the place she'd been standing when she disappeared. "He was right to send you. I'll have to tell him she's dead."

"Don't think about it now."

"I'll think about it every day for the rest of my life." I nodded at the blowtorch. "Ready?"

He fired it up. It looked like the kind chefs used to burn the sugar on crème brulees.

"Hold the pendant and use it to lift the chain. It's going to get hot."

I shuddered when Poe slipped a finger between the necklace and my skin.

"And Hallie, I didn't mean anything I said. You know that, yeah?"

"I do."

"I'm glad you two found each other, jealous even, except for the circumstances. Your grandchildren will never tire of the stories."

The hiss of the blowtorch kept me from any commentary. The chain was unbearably hot, and the second I felt it give, I jerked it off my neck. "Thank you."

"Least I could do." Poe gave me a quick kiss on top of the head and disappeared into the cabin.

"What are you going to do with it?" Dune slid his phone back in his pocket and leaned against the railing.

"Get rid of it." It was about an inch and a half long, with flower detailing, and an empty setting meant for a stone. Morning sunlight shone off the metal and I caught a hint of shadow. "It's two pieces. Should I open it?"

"If you want to." He nodded and took a step closer. "Just be careful."

I twisted the top of the cylinder. It gave a little, so I applied more force. The lid came off. "There's something inside."

Shaking, I emptied the contents into my palm. An hourglass, no bigger than a safety pin. It hummed against my skin.

Dune stared at it for a long moment before meeting my eyes.

"Mom implied I needed this to transfer abilities. I believe you're looking at the result of your quest," I whispered.

"No." He shook his head. "My quest led me to you."

I slid the hourglass back into its secret home and replaced the lid.

"You sure you don't want it?" I dangled the pendant from the chain, studying his face.

"I already have everything I want."

I kissed him, long and hard. Together we walked to the boat railing.

I balled the chain and pendant up, made a wish, and threw them both into the Mississippi.

Dune, March

I met her in front of Saint Louis Cathedral. "Hurry!" Hallie dragged me across Jackson Square. "They've been waiting for twenty minutes already."

"I told you I forgot my wallet and had to go back to the apartment. This is way different from the first time you saw them."

"Heck, yeah! We're planning a trip to Hawaii." She tugged on my hand a little harder. "I'm excited, and you're as slow as molasses."

"You're on the phone or video chat with Em or Lily every day, and you have been for the past three months. We didn't decide on Hawaii until last week. What were you all talking about all the other times?"

"Hush."

She silenced me with a kiss, but I started up again as soon as it was over.

"You didn't give in and tell them about your Newcomb acceptance, did you?" I asked.

"No. Did you tell them about Tulane?"

"Nope." Just Liam, but he didn't count, since the information had been part of my resignation letter. He'd given the school transfer and my new job his full blessing. Things were about to change at Chronos.

"Rip alert." Hallie squeezed my hand. "A pirate, I believe. At four o'clock. Do you see him?"

I searched the crowd. "I don't."

"Good."

Liam, Grace, Michael, and Emerson claimed the rips were back to normal, at least as normal as they'd ever been. Hallie could still see them, but only one at a time, and they only noticed her if she approached them directly.

I wasn't done with the Skroll. There were still more passages to translate. After the continuum calmed down, we'd learned that an Infinityglass had the power to return individual rips to their places in time.

"Still want to try to send one back?" I asked.

"Eventually." She gave me a shoulder bump. "But not today. You ready to steer a cruise ship with your mind?"

"I'm willing to walk on the beach with you, but only if you hold my hand."

"Deal." She turned to face me, raised up on her toes.

It didn't mater that we were on the sidewalk, in full view and in the way of locals and tourists alike. When our lips touched, I was lost to everything but her.

"Dune! Dune!" I heard my name and pulled away from Hallie. We both scanned the crowd this time.

"Nate!" He was racing across Jackson Square, faster than he should be, as usual. I didn't even attempt to be cool. A man hug and a few back slaps later, I heard Hallie clear her throat.

"I see you there." Nate's grin had cheeky written all over it as he turned toward her. "I thought my bestie was exaggerating when he told me how sexalicious you are in person. I thought you were a hottie through a computer screen."

"Nate," I warned. "I did *not* use that word."

"I think I need details of this conversation," Hallie said.

"Wouldn't take very much to persuade me to give them to you."

"Stop. Now." I tried for stern, but my face gave me away. "I'll tell my secrets when I'm ready."

"I'm Nate." He held out his hand. "And I know all his secrets, in case you're ready before he is."

"I'm Hallie. When do I get to see your dance moves?"

"B-boy. More tricks than moves." He did a couple, and the crowd around us applauded. Show-off.

"Maybe we can trade knowledge on that, too," Hallie said, after Nate finished taking his bows.

"Let's cut Dune out of the picture completely. Run away with me, and we'll live off the tips people put in our upturned fedoras."

Hallie laughed, wide open, and I watched Nate fall in love. I couldn't blame him.

"Okay, kids, let's go. Everyone's waiting. Betcha can't keep up." He took off.

"We can try." Hallie grabbed my hand.

When we reached Café du Monde, we found Em, Michael, Kaleb, Lily, Nate, Ava, and Poe at an outside table. All seven of them were covered in varied amounts of powdered sugar.

"You're here!" Em dropped her beignet but held on to her coffee as Hallie hugged her. Lily, less sugary than everyone else, was next.

Once they'd settled down, I pointed to the only girl still seated. "This is Ava."

"Hi, Ava." Hallie knew about Ava's past with Jack. She'd been the one to insist that Nate and Ava be a part of the Hawaii trip, claiming everyone who'd been affected by him deserved a vacation. "I heard you dance, too. Pointe?"

"Mostly contemporary." Ava's hands twisted in her lap, and she looked like she didn't know what to do once the words were out.

"You know, I love contemporary." Hallie took the empty seat next to Ava. "You'll have to come to my studio for a dance play date. If that doesn't sound lame."

"It doesn't. It sounds like . . . fun." An Ava smile was a rare thing, but Hallie scored one. A few short months ago, Hallie had been the quiet girl at the table. Now she was taking the initiative to draw Ava out.

Kaleb cleared his throat, redirecting the conversation, probably to spare Ava. "My dad says hello, and 'sends his regrets' for the Hawaii trip. Mom's at ninety-nine percent, and he's not willing to risk the remaining one. Neither am I, and not just so I can take Lily for long walks on the beach without supervision."

Lily rolled her eyes, but followed up with a kiss to Kaleb's cheek.

"Down two chaperones." Nate gave a fist pump. "I like it."

"No," Em said. "Down four. Dru's doctor doesn't want her to travel, so she and Thomas are staying home so she can rest up before her due date next month."

Michael and Emerson exchanged a look that wasn't hard to decode. Endless, unelectrified nature in Hawaii meant a lot of opportunities for two people who couldn't touch without setting off sparks.

"I think as long as we avoid wayward tiki idols and hungry sharks, we'll be fine." Michael swiped the last beignet from the paper plate on the table. "Now we just have to talk plane tickets."

"I have a solution for that, but it comes with a complication." Hallie said. "Dad wants to pay for all of them, but only if he gets to come, too."

No one said anything for a few seconds. Then Nate let out a whoop.

"Please and thank you, yes!" He stood up and did some sort of hip move that looked painful and obscene at the same time. "I'm an orphan, you know. Please, please let Daddy Warbucks know that if he needs a son, I'm not of legal age for two and-a-half more years. I could grow into a strapping young man."

"You'd have to eat a cow a day to come anywhere close to strapping." I held up my hands when Nate used the empty paper plate as a frisbee and aimed it toward my head. He missed, and a shower of powdered sugar headed for Ava.

Poe jumped out of his seat and took most of it in the chest.

"Did I stop it?" he asked her. "I tried."

"I'm fine, but you're kind of a mess." Ava grabbed a couple of napkins and tried to help him clean up, but ended up making it worse.

"Believe it or not, the mess is bigger on the inside. Kind of like the TARDIS."

When Ava laughed, Poe stared at her as if he'd been struck dumb.

There was a *moment.* My suspicions were confirmed when Hallie's elbow slammed into my ribs.

"We obviously need more beignets." I pulled Hallie out of her seat. "This round's on me."

She managed to wait until we were out of earshot. Probably. "Did you see that? With Ava and Poe?"

"I can barely breathe from the elbow jab you gave me, so yes."

"I can't believe this is my life," she said. "It's like one of those teen shows with superpowers and pretty people. And kissing. Lots of kissing."

"Happy?" I asked.

"You don't even know." Joy lit her eyes. "I have everything I've ever wanted. Almost."

I knew she was thinking about her mother.

"I'm learning to let go. Looking forward to the future. To our future."

I took stock as the bells of the Saint Louis Cathedral pealed through the spring air.

My friends sat at the table, still laughing over the powdered sugar explosion.

Less than a mile away, the Mississippi flowed, holding secrets and sorrows, buried for eternity. Gone, but not forgotten, like so many people I'd loved.

Hallie stood by my side. My reason for breathing, and the answer to every question I'd ever have.

"I couldn't be happier," I said.

And this was only the beginning.

Epilogue

Emerson, Late April

"*A*re you okay now?"

Michael held out a bottle of cold water, careful not to touch my skin. A hospital wasn't a good place to set off an electrical current. I took the water, and like the two previous bottles, stuck it down the back of my shirt.

"Childbirth is supposed to be hard on the mother. Not the aunt. If I passed out for this baby's birth, how am I ever going to manage having any of my own?"

"Knowing you, by sheer will and force of determination," he said mildly. "We'll deal with it when it happens."

"We will, will we?" I grinned at him.

We both knew it was only a matter of time.

"Is there a baby?" Kaleb burst through the waiting room doors with Lily behind him. "Is it here?"

"There's been a baby for months, and don't call it an it,"

I snapped. Fainting made me grumpy.

"You just did." Kaleb cocked his head to the side.

Lily sat down beside me and lifted my hair off my neck with one hand, fanning me with the other. "You know Thomas and Dru won't tell anyone if the baby is a girl or a boy. It's not Em's fault."

"You're too good for him, you know," I said to Lily with a sniff, but I winked at Kaleb.

He flipped me off, but he was smiling.

"Why are you so excited, Kaleb?" I asked. "Babies don't seem like your thing."

"Neither do cookies, but you don't complain about those."

A door opened and a nurse stuck her head out. "Ready to meet your newest family member?"

My stomach tried to take a vacation by way of my mouth. "As I'll ever be."

"Thomas and Dru asked for all of you." The nurse stepped back so we could enter the birthing room.

I wanted to take Michael's hand, but I crossed my arms over my chest instead.

Dru's face shone radiant, and my brother was so puffed up with pride I half expected him to pop.

"Emerson," Dru said, "meet your niece. Clarissa Elisabeth."

"After Mom." I looked at Thomas, and couldn't stop the tears from falling. He had a few of his own.

"And you," he said.

And me.

"Do you want to hold her?" Dru asked.

"I . . . I don't know. What if I break her?"

"You won't." Michael's smile of encouragement was all I needed.

I bit my lip and stepped up to the bedside, psyching myself up. "Okay."

Dru held a bundle of blanket and baby out to me, and I took her in my arms. She was beautiful, tiny, and perfect.

"Hello, Clarissa Elisabeth," I whispered. "Welcome to the world."

I bent down to place a kiss on her forehead.

And started laughing when every light bulb in the room blew.

Acknowledgments

Thank you to:

Amazing Literary Agent Holly Root, for being there at every turn, especially the sharp ones. You are the best.

Fab Film Agent Brandy Rivers, who's always excited about my work, and always an advocate.

Egmont USA, for all you've done for the HOURGLASS series and for me, and to Regina and Katie, for being the best trip chaperones a girl could have.

Stephanie Perkins, I don't think I'd have made it this year if you hadn't been in my corner. You are the truest blessing to come from this book! TWYLA FOREVER.

Jeanette Arnold and Christian Steele, you've been my anchors in reality. I am so grateful for you both, and for Maddy, Lauren, Samuel, Landon, and Mia, who shared you with me.

Critters and friends who went SO far above and beyond: Sonia

Gensler, Jodi Meadows, Natalie Parker, and Lauren Thoman. I owe you more than I'll ever be able to repay. I'm serious.

Jodi Meadows, M.G. Buehrlen, and C.J. Redwine, for always being my Go To group when it comes to the big decisions and the teensy ones. You are my sanity and my safety, and I love you dearly.

Courtney C. Stevens, C.J. Schooler, Ariel Lawhon, Angie Cardwell, and Joanna Nash, for listening ears and good advice.

Jessica Katina and the rest of the Katina family, who answered every single question about Samoa I asked, and who are lovely humans in general.

Lo, for the playlist; and Christina, for the charm offensive, and to both (Christina Lauren) for keeping me laughing. Always with the laughing, these two.

My Texas ladies: you know who you are. Special thanks to Kate Johnston, for reading on the fly; Anna Carey, for handling my weird stress sleep noises; Tara Hudson and Amy Plum, for understanding; Tessa Gratton, for buckling down with me and commiserating; Carrie Ryan and Brenna Yovanoff, for the wisdom; Gretchen McNeil, this hobo's for you; and Beth Revis, for being the best. Cheerleader. Ever.

Heather Palmquist-Lindahl, please forgive me for forgetting to add you last time!

Tammy Jones (who proves old friends are the best friends) for reading, encouraging me, and schlepping me all over NOLA in her Beetle Bug convertible.

Judith and Tom at Octavia Books in New Orleans, for inviting me to their amazing store, and for helping me see NOLA the way I needed to see it.

The Southern Independent Booksellers Alliance, and every sales rep, bookstore employee, and book pusher. Thank you for promoting literacy every day.

Every blogger who's posted a review, every reader who's used the superpower of Word of Mouth to share book love, and especially every librarian who's perfectly matched readers with my books.

Team Root, the best group of agent mates out there.

Sophie Riggsby and Jen Lamoureux, for taking care of Murphy's Law and me.

Deborrah and Keith McEntire, and Elton, Mandy, and Carter, because family is important.

My parents, Wayne and Martha Simmons, for always making sure I had a book in my hand, and for letting me read whenever I wanted. (Even in the shower.) I love you both.

Andrew and Charlie, who put up with a lot while I wrote this book (three different times), and who loved me through it anyway. Being present for the real people I love is so much more important than any work of fiction. Life is a process, and we learn as we go. I love you.

Ethan, who did way too much single-parenting in the past twelve months. You're my partner and my best friend, and I am so grateful for you (even though you're bugging me about what we're having for dinner as I type this).

It's hard to say goodbye to my Hourglass characters, but I've given them the best stories I could. They belong to the readers now, and I hope you all enjoy them!